Keshava

A Magnificent Obsession

BHAWANA SOMAAYA

BEL!EF

Published by
FiNGERPRINT! BEL!EF
An imprint of Prakash Books India Pvt. Ltd.

113/A, Darya Ganj, New Delhi-110 002,
Tel: (011) 2324 7062 – 65, Fax: (011) 2324 6975
Email: info@prakashbooks.com/sales@prakashbooks.com

facebook www.facebook.com/fingerprintpublishing
twitter www.twitter.com/FingerprintP
www.fingerprintpublishing.com

ISBN: 978 93 8777 939 6

Processed & printed in India

To all the

Radhas and the *Rukminis,*

all the gopalas and the gopikas who reside
in us after so many centuries…

Acknowledgements

Manjulika Jhaver, for introducing me to Tulsi; her passion and research got me thinking about the herbal plant and later, other chapters.

Vrinda, for being there for me when I needed to clear my thoughts; Manini and Rahul for tracing the shlokas; my editor Vidya Sury for her precision and flawless communication, and my agent Mita Kapur for believing in the concept.

CONTENTS

Chapter I: Keshava   17

Lord Krishna, lovingly called Keshava, is the most
charismatic deity of Hindu mythology and remains a
magnificent obsession for everyone and everything
associated with him—humans, plants, trees, flowers,
and objects.

Chapter II: Mayurakhi   33

Some say that Sri Krishna wears the peacock feather
because it is a symbol of illusion and he is an illusion.
Legend has it that Lord Krishna wears the peacock feathers
to wish Lord Skanda success in all endeavours.

Chapter III: Bansuri   51

Krishna's beloved Radha and gopikas are envious of
Kaanha's bansuri because the flute is forever on his lips
and when not being touched by the Lord, she is tied to his
waistband.

Chapter IV: Kadamba Tree 71

The Kadamba Tree is symbolic of romance because it was beneath the Kadamba Tree in Vrindavan that Radha and Kaanha spent time together.

Chapter V: Kamala 89

Some say the lotus flower came to be associated with Krishna after he became Dwarkadhish but folklore and ancient paintings reveal that Kaanha always loved the Kamala and used it as a metaphor to impart his teachings.

Chapter VI: Tulsi 107

Tulsi plant, associated with Lord Vishnu, is the centre of Vaishnavite worship, the manifestation of God in the plant world.

Chapter VII: Kamadhenu 159

The cows and the calves follow Kaanha wherever he
goes and all of Gokula and Vrindavan love them as their
children, which is the reason Kamadhenu is revered as
the wish-fulfilling cow in mythology.

Chapter VIII: Shankha 183

When Kaanha departs from Gokula to meet King Kamsa
in Mathura, Radha snatches his bansuri from him in the hope
that he would return to Vrindavan to get his flute from her.
He never does and after he turns an emperor, the conch
replaces the flute in his life.

Chapter IX: Peepala Tree

Lord Krishna breathes his last sitting beneath the Peepala tree, ever since regarded as a tree of worship in Hindu religion. He returns from the Yadav yatra when a tribal, mistaking him for a beast, shoots an arrow into his foot.

Foreword

Life has a bond with nature and every time there is decay and deterioration in the environment, it is a signal that humans are losing contact with the laws of nature.

There is a reason why our seers chose to go to the mountains for meditation, a reason why our ancestors exercised the bhoomi vandan, the sun worship, the watering of the Tulsi plant.

Human life does not and cannot live in isolation. All the components of universal life are inter-related and inter-dependent and mythology is proof of that.

All our deities were assigned specific animals as vehicles. As a result, Lord Indra travelled via Airavata, the elephant and Lord Kartikeya rode his peacock. Lord Ganesha, despite his potbelly, chose the mouse as his friend and Lord Shiva's constant companion is Nandi, the bullock.

The deities have their favourite flowers and plants as well and religion does not permit a devotee to mix the flower in devotion to another. So the red shoe-flower is for Lord Ganesha, the betel leaf for Lord Hanuman, white flowers for Lord Shiva, and the lotus for Lord Krishna.

Our seers emphasised that religion is science and our deities taught us by example to revere nature. The grain that nourishes our body, the herbs that heal, the trees that store our waters, bear us fruits, and offer us the wood we use for our fuel and dwelling; the same trees also provide us shade and are home to birds and animals.

Tree and animal veneration in India has been practiced since ancient times…perhaps even before the civilisation of Mohenjo-daro. Our ancestors, through practice and faith have, over the centuries, inculcated in us the habit of revering plants, trees, the ocean, the cow, the sun, and the moon.

The favours we receive from the universe are innumerable; in fact we breathe because nature exists.

Keshava: A Magnificent Obsession is about Sri Krishna's relationship with nature; the tree, the plant, the flower, the flute, the cow, and the conch, and inadvertently, with all of us breathing humans.

There's something about Sri Krishna that makes everyone who comes into contact with him—consciously or subconsciously—become consumed by him. He becomes the centre of their existence.

This includes all the men who touched his life, beginning with his biological father Vasudeva, his surrogate father Nandlal, his brother Balarama, his sakha Sudama, his companion Uddhava, his uncle Kamsa, his protégée, Arjuna, and his sons Samba and Pradyumna.

All the women in his life, his mothers Devaki and Yashoda, all the gopikas, his beloved Radha, his innumerable wives, especially Rukmini and Satyabhama, his soul mate Draupadi, sister Subhadra, and aunts Kunti and Gandhari consistently look up to him for protection and guidance.

Each and every one associated with Sri Krishna believes that their relationship with the deity is unique, which explains why every gopika felt that the Lord was only dancing with her at the Maharaas.

That is Sri Krishna's magic and also his power. He has that effect on not just humans but on everything on the planet—both living and non-living.

Keshava: A Magnificent Obsession is the story of these special bindings, stories of passion, stories of submission, stories of devotion, and of uncontainable desire.

Bhawana Somaaya

संबाधे सुरभिणा-
मंबामायासयन्तमनुयान्तीम् ।
लंबालकमवलम्बे
तं बालं तनुविलग्न जंबाव्म् ॥

**I rely entirely on that child Krishna who tires his
mother following him among the herd of cows
He has long hair and his body is covered with mud**

13

अश्रितपिञ्छापीडं
वञ्चितसौजन्यवल्लवीवलयम् ।
अधरमणिनिहितवेणुं
बालं गोपालमनिशमवलम्बे ॥

I rely entirely on child Krishna who adorns
his head with peacock plumes
He is surrounded by loving cowherd belles
whom he dodges
And he plays the flute placing it on
his jewel-like lips

प्रह्लादभागधेयं
निगममहाद्रेर्गुहान्तराधेयम् ।
नरहरिपदाभिधेयं
विबुधविधेयं ममानुसन्धेयम् ॥

I meditate on Krishna, who is the
good fortune of Prahlada
He is sought after in the caves of the Vedas which
are like huge mountains
He is named Narahari meaning having a form
which is part man part lion
And who helps devas

Keshava

Lord Krishna, lovingly called Keshava, is the most charismatic deity of Hindu mythology and remains a magnificent obsession for everyone and everything associated with him—humans, plants, trees, flowers, and objects.

CHAPTER 1

Keshava

Lord Krishna, lovingly called Keshava, is the most charismatic deity of Hindu mythology and remains a magnificent obsession for everyone and everything associated with him—humans, plants, trees, flowers, and objects.

Keshava

A MAGNIFICENT OBSESSION

यथाकाशस्थितो नित्यं वायुः सर्वत्रगो महान् ।
तथा सर्वाणि भूतानि मत्स्थानीत्युपधारय ॥

The sky is rigid in its position
The air even though fickle does not let go of its place
In the end, all living planets have to reside within me

I am Krishna.

I am Keshava.

People call me by different names in different regions.

For some I am Vishnu.

For some I am Ayyappa.

In different eras and different faiths my names alter, but not my faith.

I am Achala.

I am Adbhuta.

I am Aditya.

I am Ajaya.

Those who seek me, those who submit to me know that I am the middle as well as the end of the sky and other parts of nature; in short, every creation, sustenance, or destruction is a part of my magnificence.

I am the knowledge...I am the awareness...I am the conflict in times of despair.

I am the shape in the alphabet spread out in the scriptures.

In grammar I am the adjective, the preposition, the noun, and the adverb.

In tense, I am the past, the present, as well as the future.

In the cycle of Karma, I am the provider and also the receiver.

In times of injustice, I am the oppressor so that those without values learn righteousness.

I am greed, I am ambition, and I am also success.

I am silence that preserves secrets and also knowledge that spreads awareness.

Some call me Achyuta, the infallible.

Some call me Adidev, the original.

Some address me as Ajanma, the unborn.

Some name me Akshara, the indestructible.

I am all of this and none of this.

I am faith.

I am perception.

I am Krishna.

Chaturbhuja

LORD ARMED WITH FOUR HANDS

यो मां पश्यति सर्वत्र सर्वं च मयि पश्यति ।
तस्याहं न प्रणश्यामि स च मे न प्रणश्यति ॥

**One who turns to me and searches
for everything inside me I am never far away
from them and them from me**

It is their infinite love for me that my devotees describe
me in superlatives.

For them I am Amrit, the nectar.

I am Anandsagar...trancendental bliss.

I am Ananta...endless.

I am Ananya...one who has no leader.

I don't come from the North.

I don't come from the West.

I have not emerged from down South.

Nor invaded from the East.

I don't hail from the top.

I don't spring from below.

I don't come from any direction.

Actually I don't come at all.
I am Aparajita, who cannot be defeated.
I am Avyukta, who is crystal clear.
I am Krishna.

◦❧ I.3 ❧◦

Devadideva

GOD OF GODS

नियतं कुरु कर्म त्वं कर्म ज्यायो ह्यकर्मणः ।
शरीरयात्रापि च ते न प्रसिद्ध्येदकर्मणः ॥

**Our scriptures define niyati as predestined
It means that we follow what is in store for us
Unless we do so we cannot forsake
Our body when the time comes**

We are all projections of other people's perceptions. I am no exception.

Some perceive me as a child avatar. For them I am Balagopala, Balakrishna.

Some view me as an eternal traveller. For them I am Banke Bihari.

I was always there and will continue to be there.

When I renounce my body the surviving part of me will prevail amongst the five ingredients of nature.

The sixth will be the heart of human beings.

I will be drawn to anyone who pulls me in in his direction and provides me space in his heart.

I am Danavendra, assigned to grant boons to the deserving.

I am Dharadhyaksha, committed to justice.

~ I.4 ~

Gyaneshwara

LORD OF KNOWLEDGE

कालोऽस्मि लोकक्षयकृत्प्रवृद्धो-
लोकान्समाहर्तुमिह प्रवृत्तः ।
ऋतेऽपि त्वां न भविष्यन्ति सर्वे
येऽवस्थिताः प्रत्यनीकेषु योधाः ॥

The sun rises and sets
At the allotted time
The human body must renounce
The world when time beckons

I am a lover of cowherds.

I am Gopalpriya.

I am Lord of all senses.

I am Hrushikesha.

I am the creator of the golden womb.

I am Hiranyagarbha.

I have narrated in the Bhagavad Gita that among the elephants I am Airavata, among trees I am Peepala, among the rivers I am Ganga and among the cows I am Kamadhenu.

Among the birds I am partial to the peacock. I have adorned the peacock feather in my crown forever but have never been able to unravel the mystery of its myriad colours.

Is the colour of the peacock feather blue-brown layered with purple or is it grey-silver layered with black?

Is it all these colours combined or is there more?

Are these colours of passion…of desire…or desolation?

Among the plants I am enamoured by Tulsi and devoted to her virtue. Tulsi is dignity and it is my promise to her that my worship will be incomplete without a leaf from her plant.

Among the flowers I admire the lotus because it rises in muddy water but remains sacred.

I am Jagdisha.

I am Jagadguru.

I am Janardan.

I am Jagannatha.

I am Keshava

Innumerable names but one common force, devotion.

Kamalanayana

ONE WITH LOTUS EYES

नैनं छिन्दन्ति शस्त्राणि नैनं दहति पावकः ।
न चैनं क्लेदयन्त्यापो न शोषयति मारुतः ॥

अच्छेद्योऽयमदाह्योऽयमक्लेद्योऽशोष्य एव च ।
नित्यः सर्वगतः स्थाणुरचलोऽयं सनातनः ॥

जातस्य हि ध्रुवो मृत्युर्ध्रुवं जन्म मृतस्य च ।
तस्मादपरिहार्येऽर्थे न त्वं शोचितुमर्हसि ॥

अव्यक्तादीनि भूतानि व्यक्तमध्यानि भारत ।
अव्यक्तनिधनान्येव तत्र का परिदेवना ॥

Weapons cannot pierce through his soul
Fire cannot burn it
Water cannot drench it
The wind cannot dry it
The soul is eternal
Cannot be damaged, burnt, or drowned

It is ageless, timeless and eternal
The one who is born has to die
The one who dies has to be reborn
It's futile to mourn transitory

The soul has no image, no attachment
It is disconnected
From the cycle of life and death
Unlike the body
It watches the body embroil
In the maze of desire and hope
Aware that it is all futile and transitory

It does not matter that I am Yashoda's lalla, the heir of Vasudeva and Devaki. It does not natter that I am brother of Subhadra and Balarama, friend of Draupadi and guide of Arjuna.

I will remain the heartbeat of Gokula and Vrindavan, the messiah of Mathura and the caretaker of Dwarka.

Some call me a cowherd, some a manipulator, some a miracle worker.

I am Keshava.

I am Kaanha.

I am Krishna.

I am the beloved of Radha and the gopikas, the companion of the gwalas and the consort of queens Rukmini and Satyabhama.

I am associated with celebration and colours...green for spring...yellow for my pitambar...blue for the colour of my skin...red for passion.

There are so many stories...the adventure of river Yamuna and later Govardhan mountain, the victory with Sheshnaag...

I cherish these memories like I cherish the peacock feather I always adorn in my crown.

I value nature for giving in abundance to the universe and want to give back as much as I receive.

I value the Tulsi plant and its healing nature. Tulsi is tradition, she is mother Goddess and she is my earthly consort.

I admire the flute... its sacrifice and endurance. Without suffering there is no creation, without hardship there is no melody. The bansuri submits to a bigger cause and that is why it is precious to me. Not every tree can create a flute.

I love the Kadamba tree...I love its generosity and compassion. The Kadamba tree is a witness to many secrets, so many romances but she never betrays and never tires of listening.

I love the Kamala...the lotus flower is strong and silent. She blossoms in stench yet preserves her purity. She radiates fragrance, she is our Karma.

I love the peacock, its varied colours, there's a mystery about it like there's a mystery about life.

I am incomplete without Kamadhenu...my cows and their offspring follow me silently wherever I go. They inspire faith. They shower love without expectations. Kamadhenu is contentment.

I salute the shankha, always geared up for a new start and new vibrations. The conch spreads good will, is positive, peaceful, auspicious, and therefore a part of my worship.

I am indebted to the Peepala tree, it is here I embarked on my samadhi and Peepala engulfed me like a mother wraps her child in her lap. It soaked up my suffering, calmed my anxieties, and bid me a peaceful farewell. Under its shade and rhythmic flutter I dropped my defences and meditated...

The Peepala tree inspires detachment. Every day, so many voyagers rest beneath its shade, yet the tree never counts its good deeds. Every day, so many leaves fall off its branches, yet the tree never mourns the loss. It is always ready for another traveller, another sunrise.

I define the uplifting Tulsi, the magnificent bansuri.

I define the blossoming Kadamba, the fragrant Kamala.

The wish fulfilling Kamadhenu, the auspicious shankha, and the fluttering Peepala as the eight wonders of nature that resides within me.

I am because they are...!

संसारे किं सारं
कंसारेश्शरणकमलपरिभजनम् ।
ज्योतिः किमन्धकारे
यदन्धकारेरनुस्मरणम् ॥

What is the essence of this samsara?
It is worshipping the lotus feet of the enemy of Kamsa
What is light in darkness?
Thinking of the enemy of Krishna

कलशनवनीतचोरे
कमलादृक्कुमुदचन्द्रिकापूरे ।
विहरतु नन्दकुमारे
चेतो मम गोपसुन्दरीजारे ॥

Let my mind revel in the son of Nanda who is the
paramour of the gopis
He steals fresh butter from the pot
He is like moonlight for the lily-like eyes of Lakshmi

कस्त्वं बालः बलानुजः किमिह ते मन्मन्दिराशङ्कया
युक्तं तन्नवनीतपात्रविवरे हस्तं किमर्थं न्यसेः ।
मातः कञ्चन वत्सकं मृगयितुं मागा विषादं क्षणा-
दित्येवं वरवल्लवीप्रतिवचः कृष्णस्य पुष्णातु नः ॥

This is a conversation between a gopi and child
Krishna who is caught red-handed while stealing
butter in her house

Gopi: Who are you, child?
Krishna: I am the younger brother of Balarama
Gopi: Why are you here?
Krishna: I thought that this was my house
Gopi: And why did you put your hands inside the pot
of butter placed on the top?
Krishna: Mother, I was searching for a calf,
please do not worry

May these replies of Krishna to the queries of the gopi
nurture and protect us!

CHAPTER II

Mayurakhi

Some say that Sri Krishna wears the peacock feather because
it is a symbol of illusion and he is an illusion. Legend has
it that Lord Krishna wears the peacock feathers to wish
Lord Skanda success in all endeavours.

CHAPTER 14

Jayrakhi

Some say that Sri Krishna wears the peacock feather because it is a symbol of illusion and he is an illusion. Legend has it that Lord Krishna wears the peacock feather to wish Lord Skanda success in all endeavours.

Mayurakhi

I AM FASTENED TO MY LORD'S CROWN

अभिनवनवनीतस्निग्धमापीतदुग्धं
दधिकणपरिदिग्धं मुग्धमंगं मुरारेः ।
दिशतु भुवनकृच्छ्रच्छेदि तापिञ्छगुच्छ-
च्छवि नवशिखिपिञ्छलाञ्छितं वाञ्छितं नः ॥

**May Lord Krishna grant us our wishes; Krishna
whose pretty body, nurtured by drinking milk, is as
smooth as freshly prepared butter and is smeared all
over with drops of curd, which destroys the suffering
of the three worlds, which is dark blue as the
Tapinjha flowers, and is adorned with the fresh
plumes of a peacock**

I am Mayura.

I am Peacock.

I am fastened to my Lord's crown and watch the world
spin by. He never removes me from his hair band and I like
to believe that because I am close to his head, I am forever
in his mind.

Mother Yashoda says that I suit her Lalla's crown because we have blue in common. He wears yellow pitambar but is always addressed as Niladri. I reflect multiple colours. I am always described in shades of blue.

I hail from India, from Sri Lanka, from Myanmar, from Indochina, from Java, and also from Africa. Those unfamiliar with me cannot tell the difference but we instantly know when we have a migrant amidst us. Their plumages are of different shades and while all of us are genetically vain our temperaments vary drastically.

The Congo peacocks display their tails during courtship. Their feathers are comparatively shorter and their colours don't sparkle in the way I shine when I dance in the sun.

I am attractive and I know it, I am aware that my beauty casts a spell around me and I enjoy flaunting my long tail quill feathers whenever I have an audience because I love being watched.

My counterpart, the peahen, is not as boastful as me and it is also because her plumage is not as radiant as mine and her colours, a mixture of dull grey, brown, and green can never have the effect I have on my surrounding. She accepts my superiority and shies away from attention. She hides when she is being watched and the only time she displays her plumage is to ward off female competition or to signal danger to her young ones.

When she is around I need not worry because she will guard me and all around her. Our chicks of both sexes and in all the species are cryptically coloured and vary between yellow and tawny, usually with patches of darker brown or light tan and ivory.

Our chicks change and alter colours as they grow up.

I am Annamayil.

I am Arju.

I am recognized as much for my beauty as for my vocals. I sing to attract peahens. I sing when I am mating, I sing just when I am about to mate, I sing during copulation, and I sing post mating. I sing because I like singing and because I love my voice.

I like dancing too and prance in the gardens when I am rejoicing or when I sense a climate change. I am attracted to the skyline, drawn to the clouds, and love the rains. When I dance I am joined by my friends and poets wait in the dark to watch the celebration. That is how so many songs and verses have been written about us.

I reside in the forest amidst lush trees. I love the density and the quietude around me. I tread softly on the grass and pluck on the plants, sometimes flower petals, seed heads, insects, and whatever I find and I believe they like me to hover around them. I go searching for food at dawn or at dusk and stroll around leisurely until I am satiated and only then do I retreat to my shade and security.

Most of us wander in the wilderness but some of us, the domesticated ones, live in orchards or magnificent gardens and alter our lifestyles according to our masters, and therefore survive on bread and cracked grain, sometimes oats and corn, sometimes cheese, cooked rice, and sometimes, cat food.

Like humans I crave for protein rich food that includes meat, vegetables, leafy greens, broccoli, carrots, beans, beets, peas, and fruits, but I am too arrogant to go searching for them and expect that it will somehow find a way towards me and it does, maybe that is the reason I am also referred to as the royal bird!

I am regal; I know there is grandeur about me.

I am Chandrak.

I am Ghanapriya.

I am connected to the moon; I am connected to the clouds, to the rains. Nobody clearly remembers how I came into existence many, many centuries ago but there are many fascinating tales.

I am told I was the vehicle of Lord Kartikeya, the God of war. I am told that Kartikeya split the demon king, Surapadman into two and converted the two parts into an integral part of him, one manifesting into a peacock, his mount, and another, a rooster adorning his flag.

In the coming yug I was transformed into the crown of Lord Krishna, an avatar of Lord Vishnu, the reason he is addressed as Mayur Pankhi. I am privileged that Lord Krishna forever wears my feather in his crown and is associated with my name, Mormukatdhari. I have never told this to him but I truly believe that my feather adds splendour to his persona. There is nobody as magnificent as him.

My forefathers reveal that there is a story of how Lord Krishna came to be associated with the title, Mormukatdhari. As per the legend, one day, my Lord, tired after a hard day's work, was resting in the forest with his cowherd friends, when he suddenly woke up from his slumber and started playing his flute like he was in a trance.

Slowly, the effect of the music emanating from the flute engulfed his entire surroundings. The fatigued cowherds resting around him woke up raptured by the melody and remained in a trance.

At a distance, the cows were grazing but suddenly lost interest and bells clanging around their necks, rushed to follow the sound of the music and to return to where Lord Krishna was seated beneath a tree.

The music floated through the forest and the trees, through the streams, and the flower buds and all the peacocks, so far in hiding, emerged from the bushes and began flapping their wings. The grey blue brown peacocks were jumping in joy and singing together. They continued to dance as long as Krishna continued to play the flute! The sky was shining, the sun was smiling and the stars were set for a long journey at dusk.

वेणीमूले विरचित घनश्यामपिञ्छावचूडो
विद्युल्लेखावलयित इव स्निग्धपीतांबरेण ।
मामालिङ्गन्मरतकमणिस्तंभगंभीरबाहुः
स्वप्ने दृष्टस्तरुणतुलसीभूषणो नीलमेघः ॥

I dreamed that Krishna was embracing me with his majestic hands resembling pillars of emerald, wearing garlands of fresh tulsi leaves, and his complexion dark as

the clouds. His hair was adorned with peacock plumes
dark as the cloud and he was wearing bright yellow
robes which gave the impression that he was
enveloped by streaks of lightning

~ II.2 ~

Tapinjha

I WARD OFF EVIL AND BRING GOOD LUCK

यां दृष्ट्वा यमुनां पिपासुरनिशं व्यूहो गवां गाहते
विद्युत्वानिति नीलकण्ठनिवहो
यां द्रष्टुमुत्कण्ठते ।
उत्तंसाय तमालपल्लवमिति छिन्दन्ति यं गोपिकाः
कान्तिः
कालियशासनस्य वपुषः सा पावनी पातु नः ॥

The dark complexion of Krishna causes confusion in the
minds of cows and thinking that it is the river Yamuna—
also dark—they enter into it to quench their thirst.
The peacocks think that it is a dark cloud and are
raring to see it. The milkmaids think it is the tender leaf
of the Tamala tree and pluck it to adorn their
hair. May that purifying lustre of the discipline
of Kaliya—Krishna—protect us!

There was peace and serenity all around and everyone could hear the sound of the waterfall: the echoes across the mountains, the buzzing bees and the singing birds, all the living planets were in one place and everyone was celebrating, it was as if time stood still!

Peacocks like to dance to express their joy and we danced collectively, vigorously. Our ancestors had never experienced such bliss, this was a sublime experience and in their trance travelled to the lotus feet of Sri Krishna and requested my Lord to dance with him.

My Lord can never refuse a devotee and joined my vibrant friends, continuing to play his flute. The faster we danced, the quicker he tapped his fingers on the bamboo. Something magical was happening and it was evident in the energy exuded in the universe. The effect was overpowering and some of them unable to contain the euphoria collapsed in exhaustion!

I am Shirali.

I am Shikhandi.

I am overwhelmed by my legacy.

My forefathers share that it was an unusual day and an unusual experience. It appeared as if the dance would never end. That Lord Krishna would never stop playing the flute. But slowly the music turned feeble and gradually diminished. We had stopped dancing, stopped flapping our feathers but our reverie was yet to be broken. Our hearts were racing and our eyes were weeping…

Is this what they call ecstasy? It must be because our king bowed to the lotus feet and said he owed an offering to the Lord for this surreal experience. He kneeled before Sri Krishna and did something he had never done before. He offered a part of his opulence, his plumage as guru dakshina to his master. He bowed again and again and every time he did so, his plumages scattered on the floor creating a tapestry before the Lord.

Lord Krishna slowly rose from his trance bent and picked up all the scattered feathers from the floor, some he held in his hands and some he stuffed into his crown.

I have gone through this story again and again in my mind and often wonder, what must have happened that day? Did Sri Krishna engineer the miracle or was it a wonder beyond his realm? Did he pluck the plumage and spontaneously attach it to his crown or was there a bigger plan of the universe?

I am Arjun.

I am Lepakshi.

Some say that Sri Krishna wears the peacock feather because it is a symbol of illusion and He is an illusion. So many perceptions, so many interpretations to my colours as well, the best I have heard is about the universe covered in akasha that appears blue during the day and black at night, so does Lord Krishna. There is more. Lord Krishna, an avatar of Lord Vishnu, is the maternal uncle of Lord Skanda, the senapati whose mount is the peacock and legend says that Sri Krishna wears the peacock feathers to guard off evil and bring success to Lord Skanda in all his endeavours.

Whatever the reason, I am privileged to be in close proximity with my Lord for so many centuries.

I must be special to be bestowed this favour, actually I know I am special. When I spread my plumes into a full-blown circular form I adapt the divine shape of Omkara. In a different continent, I am the third animal zodiac sign and yes, I deliberately consume poison to sustain my immunity.

The Buddhist deity Mahamayuri is depicted seated on me. I support the throne of Amitabha, the ruby red sunset coloured archetypal Buddha of Infinite Light.

I am Kalapi.

I am Krutika.

Ancient Greeks believed that the flesh of peafowl did not decay after death, so I came to be revered as symbol of immortality, later adopted by Christianity, which is why I am visible in their paintings, mosaics, and scriptures and remain a vital part of the Easter celebrations in the east.

The "eyes" in my tail feathers symbolise the all-seeing Christian God and in some interpretations, the Church. A peacock drinking from a vase is a symbol of a Christian drinking from the waters of eternal life, in other words I symbolise the cosmos—the sun, the moon, and the stars. In other regions like Persia and Babylon, I signify the paradise and the Tree of Life.

I am immortal.

I am Pekham.

I am guardian to royalty. The first great dynasty unifying the Indian sub-continent in the third century BCE, Maurya Dynasty, named after the patriarch Chandragupta Maurya has me in their emblem. The monarchy in Iran is referred to as the Peacock Throne.

The Yazidi consider me an emanation of God. They believe that a benevolent angel created the cosmos from an egg and that the angel wept for 7,000 years and the tears were filled up in seven big jars, which eventually quenched the fires of Hell. This angel in all their arts and sculptures is depicted as a peacock.

वृन्दावनन्द्रमतलेषु गवां गणेषु
वेदावसानसमयेषु च दृश्यते यत् ।
तद्ब्रेणुवादनपरं शिखिपिञ्छचूडं
ब्रह्म स्मरामि कमलेक्षणमभ्रनीलम् ॥

That which is seen underneath the trees of Vrindavan, in the group of cows, in the concluding portions of Vedas – on that brahman I meditate, visualizing it as playing the flute, sporting a peacock feather on its head, with lotus-like eyes and dark-blue complexion of the water-charged clouds

~

~ II.3 ~

Mukuna

I AM GUARDIAN TO ROYALTY

व्यत्यस्तपादमवतंसितबर्हिबर्हं
साचीकृताननिवेशितवेणुरन्ध्रम् ।
तेजः परं
परमकारुणिकं पुरस्तात्
प्राणप्रयाणसमये मम सन्निधत्ताम् ॥

**May the resplendent form of Krishna, full of compassion
and kindness, with legs crossed, peacock feather
adorning the head, the hole of the flute placed to the
lips and with face slightly tilted to the side, be at my
bedside when life is ebbing out of this body**

Birds were strangers to Greece till the conquest of King
Alexander and myth has it that I pulled the chariot of Greek
goddess Hera. Hera had a faithful aide with hundred eyes
called Argus and his only job was to guard Io, the woman
who was transformed into a cow by Hera when she sensed
Zeus was attracted to Io. Zeus used his powers to kill Argus
through eternal sleep and liberate Io from Hera's captivity

but Hera, as tribute to her faithful watchman, preserved the hundred eyes of Argus in my, her charioteer's tail.

I am Mayil.

I am Gusana.

I am fascinated by fables around me, some make-believe and some real.

Some call me Navilla.

Some call me Neelkanth.

During the Medieval period, various types of fowls were consumed as food and these included common birds, such as the chicken. The affluent families however preferred more majestic birds like the swan and on special occasions, a peacock.

I was magnificently spread on a king's dining table more for ostentatious display and less for culinary consumption.

Some say I was revived in the Renaissance iconography that unified Hera and Juno. Maybe these are stories, I don't know. It is said that in 1956, John J. Graham created an abstraction of an eleven feathered peacock logo for American broadcaster NBC. This brightly hued peacock was adopted due to the increase in colour programming. NBC's first colour broadcasts showed only a still frame of the colourful me. The emblem made its first on-air appearance on 22 May 1956. A stylised me in full display is still the logo of our national film festivals.

I am Kekaa.

I am Mayinni.

After so many centuries, so many songs and poetry on me, the human race knows very little about me. They don't know that we are called peafowl, the male is peacock, the female peahen, the babies, peachicks, and the family is called a bevy.

They don't know that we are not born with our fancy tail feathers. The male peachicks don't start growing their showy trains until they are three years old and it's hard to decipher the sex of a peachick because they are identical to their mothers. So it's only after they grow six months old that the male chicks begin to change colour.

The humans don't know that they don't have to harm us to collect our feathers because we shed them naturally after every mating season. They don't know that we can all live harmoniously without trading upon the other.

They don't know that our average lifespan is twenty years but during the two decades, our tail feathers can reach up to six feet long and add 60 per cent of its body length.

They don't know that despite our odd proportions, we can fly, not very far, not very high, but just fine.

I am Kalgi.

I am Tawoos.

I am the blue beautiful bird. I have a slender neck and distinct voice. I tiptoe gently on the ground and spread my magnificence when I am joyous. My feathers sparkle like crystal in sunlight and my eyes shimmer in the moonlight.

I am Morra.

I am Mayurakhi.

अयि परिचिनु चेतः प्रातरंभोजनेत्रं
कबरकलितचञ्चत् पिञ्छदामाभिराममम् ।
वलभिदुपलनीलं वल्लवी भागधेयं
निखिलनिगमवल्लीमूलकन्दं मुकुन्दम् ॥

O Mind! Meditate on the form of Mukunda with eyes
beautiful as the lotus at sunrise, hair prettily done with a
garland of peacock plumes, complexion dark blue as the
sapphire, the good fortune of the gopis and the root of
all the Vedas which are like creepers

CHAPTER III

Bansuri

Krishna's beloved Radha and gopikas are envious of Kaanha's bansuri because the flute is forever on his lips and when not being touched by the Lord, she is tied to his waistband.

Murli

I AM MELODY

I am forever with Lord Krishna. I am made
out of bamboo and close to nature.

मुरलिनिनदलोलं मुग्धमायूरचूडं
दलितदनुजजालं धन्यसौजन्यलीलम् ।
परहितनवहेलं पद्मसद्मानुकूलं
नवजलधरनीलं नौमि गोपालबालम् ॥

**Behold Child Gopala who is raptured
by the music from the flute
Who wears beautiful peacock plumes on his head
and crushes hordes of asuras
Whose playful activities are charming, who does
good to others, who favours Brahma
And who is dark blue in colour as the
newly formed cloud**

I am Murli.
I am melody.
I am tranquillity.

I am ancient, I am organic and I'm the oldest among the earliest musical instruments discovered by mankind and therefore associated with Satyug and the deities.

There is mention of me in the Puranas and mention of me in the scriptures written thousands of years ago.

I am the mode of communication between Lord Krishna and his beloved Radha Rani. I am also the bone of contention between them and the reason of anxiety for Krishna's gopikas. They are all envious of me and often complain to their Lord about me.

My Lord is aware of their resentment towards me and also their attraction for me. Everyone obsessed with Kaanha nurses mixed emotions towards me because I am where they desire to be.

I understand their hostility.

There is an old folklore and I will recount it for those of you, who don't know the story.

One day, it seems, Lord Krishna asked his devotees that if given an opportunity to choose an avatar associated with him, which would they pick?

The devotees were confused as they had never dreamt of such a possibility. After great deliberation, one devotee expressed that she would like to be born as a Lotus Flower because Krishna held the flower in his hand most of the time.

Another mentioned that she would like to be incarnated as the Kadamba tree because her Lord would be seated beneath her shade in all his leisure time.

A third shared he would like to be born as the Peepala tree because that is where Krishna breathed his last. The fourth devotee opted to be reincarnated as the conch so that he would accompany his Lord during the Kurukshetra and learn so much from him.

The fifth devotee chose the Sudarshana Chakra because he wanted to watch how Krishna delivered justice. The sixth yearned to be born as the Peacock so that he could sit on Krishna's crown and travel with him where ever he went.

The seventh devotee confesed she would like to be born as the Tulsi plant and fulfil her fantasy to be married, even if it was just for a night to Lord Krishna.

Krishna heard them all out in silence and was surprised that none of his devotees' wanted to be incarnated as a flute. He was aware that everyone envied the special position the flute held in his life, yet today, when he granted them a boon to choose an avatar, none of them wanted to be reincarnated as the flute.

Why?

The devotees had no answer and Krishna did not probe them further but the thought remained with him. The thought nagged me too, I wondered why no one wanted to be born in my avatar but I had no answers.

Perhaps Sri Krishna knew but did not want to tell me, perhaps he will when the time is right. I have stopped thinking about it. Since this is the only avatar I have experienced I have no complaints. I am content just being around my Lord.

I am Murli.

I am happiness.

Many want to become me but lack the courage.

I go wherever Krishna travels or let me put it this way he never travels without me.

～๑ III.2 ๑～

Bansuri

I AM RHYTHM

I submit to my Lord. Krishna created
me and looks after me.

यद्वेणुश्रेणिरूपस्थितसुषिरमुखोद्गीर्णनादप्रभिन्ना
एणाक्ष्यस्तत्क्षणेन त्रुटितनिजपतिप्रेमबन्धा बभूवुः ।
अस्तव्यस्तालकान्ता स्फुरदधरकुचद्वन्द्वनाभिप्रदेशाः
कामावेशप्रकर्षप्रकटितपुलकाः पातु पीतांबरो नः ॥

**The moment the doe-eyed damsels of Vraja heard the
enthralling sweet melodies emanating from the
drops of Krishna's flute
The bonds of love binding them to their husbands were
cut asunder and they were hungry to join Krishna
Their lips, breasts, and navel trembled with passion
as they ran out of their homes in flying saris and**

dishevelled hair to join their Lord
May that Krishna who clothes himself in bright
yellow silks protect us forever!

I am Bansuri.

I was discovered amidst nature, created from a bamboo, and nourished in natural surroundings.

That is why every time I open my heart to express, flowers bloom, birds sing, and the skyline changes colours.

Legend has it that Lord Krishna would stroll every evening into the forest to communicate with the trees. He loved them and never failed to express his affection to all the branches and all the leaves. The trees adored him and every time he walked into the forest, they blossomed in his presence.

One day, Krishna wandered into the forest looking unusually sad. The forest sensed his desolation. Krishna walked hesitantly and stopped in front of the Bamboo plant. He caressed the bark and stood staring at it for long. The Bamboo plant was concerned; it had never seen Krishna so weighed down. "What's worrying you, my friend?" the Bamboo asked his Lord.

Krishna looked pale and choking on his words, whispered, "I have a favour to ask you, but it is not an easy one." The Bamboo said, "Express what is on your mind. If the favour is within my possibility I will grant it to you wholeheartedly."

Krishna sighed, "I need to ask you for your life, my friend. I need to cut you." The Bamboo was taken aback for a brief moment but recovered immediately and responded, "You clearly don´t have any other choice. If you did, I know you would not have asked me for this favour, right?" "No alternative at all," responded Krishna with a heavy heart. "Then so be it, what are you waiting for?" concluded the Bamboo, lowering its head before his Lord.

So Krishna axed the Bamboo, chiselled many circular holes in it, and every time he did so, the Bamboo cringed in pain. Krishna was aware of the Bamboo's suffering, aware of its agony but carried on with his task till he had created a beautiful flute out of it.

The flute was so artistic and ornate, that suddenly the Bamboo stopped crying and when Krishna placed the flute on his lips and created melody, the Bamboo was weeping in ecstasy. "Do you weep because you are hurting, my friend?" Krishna stroked the flute and wiped her tears. "I weep in gratitude, my Lord, earlier I could rest my eyes on you only when you sauntered into my forest, but now you hold me with you slender fingers, you stroke me, rest me on your lips. I am forever beside you, I feel privileged to be the chosen one."

The melody emanating from the flute was mesmerising and everyone in the village were hypnotised by the sound of the musical instrument created by Sri Krishna. Wherever he went, Keshava carried the flute with him. If he was not playing it, she was tied to his waist.

In the beginning everyone found it very charming but as time went by and Sri Krishna remained obsessed with his flute, everyone associated with him began looking upon the bansuri as an invader.

Krishna's beloved Radha Rani particularly was resentful of the flute because now she could never be alone with her Kaanha without the flute coming in the way.

Krishna's mother Yashoda was irritated with the flute too because now it was impossible to communicate with her son forever preoccupied with his bansuri. The gopikas were the most upset; earlier their Lord found some time for them but after the arrival of the flute he belonged to nobody.

Exasperated, the gopikas went marching to the forest in search of the Bamboo tree who had submitted to this exercise. They discovered a broken Bamboo tree and poured their hearts out. "Our Lord sleeps with you in his waist band, he wakes up with you on his lips, he travels with you everywhere so what is the secret? Why does he treasure you so much and ignore the rest of us?"

The Bamboo was surprised by their outburst but also flattered. He pondered for sometime and responded, "I am not certain why he treasures me so much but I suspect that the secret probably is that I'm hollow inside and easy to surrender. I have faith that whatever my Lord does is for my betterment and I submit to him and the result is before you...

"The secret perhaps is in submission...If you submit to the sound of the flute, to the Lord, you'll be drawn into the fragrance of the melody and maybe then, you will not find me invasive…"

In his discourse to his devotees, Sri Krishna emphasises the importance of the flute and draws similarities with human life. He explains that in the human body as in the flute, there are eight main spots: The five organs of perception, mind, intellect, and ego.

If you get rid of your ego and become like a hollow reed flute, then the Lord will come to you, pick you up, place you on his lips, and breathe through you. Then out of the hollowness of your heart he will create a captivating melody and consume you in his fragrance for eternity.

If you continue to wallow in self pity and encourage negativity, the Lord will distance himself from you, because in the ensuing situation, you serve no purpose to him. Or at least, that is what I have understood of my Lord.

My Lord has taught me that in giving is receiving.

I am Bansuri.

I endure, I submit, and therefore I gain.

Baanhi

I APPEAL TO COWHERDS
I am identified with Krishna rasleela.

अंसालम्बितवामकुण्डलभरं मन्दोन्नतभ्रूलतं
किञ्चित्कुञ्चितकोमलाधरपुटं साचिप्रसारेक्षणम् ।
आलोलाङ्गुलिपल्लवैर्मुरलिकामापूरयन्तं मुदा
मूले कल्पतरोस्त्रिभंगललितं जाने जगन्मोहनम् ॥

I know that Krishna, seated under the wish-giving tree
He captivates the universe by his beautiful form
His earlobes hanging down to his shoulders
His raised and curved eye brows and slightly
drawn down pretty lower lip
His eyes dancing as he plays the flute with
speedily moving fingers
As soft and red leaf buds bloom

I am Baanhi.

Some say I originated from South Asia and was identified as a musical instrument associated with the cowherds and the pastoral tradition.

I am linked to the legendary love story of Lord Krishna and Radha and also depicted in Buddhist paintings from around 100 CE.

The present generation knows me through skilled artistes who have mastered me and are custodians of music generated through me.

There are innumerable stories connected to my melody, innumerable stories of the effect it had on the Braj bhoomi, the villagers, the animals, birds, and the insects of Vrindavan.

It is said that I originated from the Sanskrit word bans- meaning bamboo and sur - meaning melody. While everyone has one family, I have two types of families: transverse and fipple.

The transverse or side-blown bamboo flute is from northern India. It is one of the world's most ancient instruments, having existed in more or less in its current form for about 4,000 years.

The fipple flute is usually played in folk music and is held at the lips like a whistle and enables superior control, variations, and embellishments.

I have many references in the Puranas and this has mainly to do with my complex structure. Not every bamboo is considered suitable to create me. I call for a thin-walled bamboo, straight with a uniform circular cross section, carrying long internodes.

It isn't that easy to find a shaft that has the requisite characteristics to create my form, which is why the old guards say that the making of a bansuri is rare and expensive.

A specific species of bamboo called Pseudostachyum is best suited to create me and I am located in the faraway forests of Assam and Kerala.

Creating me requires a specific climate and great expertise. I have to be harvested, preserved, and pampered to naturally exude resins that will strengthen my body.

Not everyone has the patience to nuture me. Only the wise and the aware can groom me, protect me. Only experts recognise when I am ripe and have the knowledge and the technique to insert a cork stopper inside me to block one end, next to which the blowing hole is burnt in.

Only trained artistes are familiar with how to delicately burn the holes with red hot skewers because drilling causes the fibrous bamboo to split along the length, rendering it useless.

I am created with a lot of patience, a lot of effort, and a lot of care.

I am Baanhi.

I am special because Krishna conceived me.

~ III.4 ~

Baashi

I SUBMIT TO MY LORD

Not everyone can figure me out. I am easy to hurt
and Krishna understands this.

लोकानुन्मदयन् श्रुतीर्मुखरयन् क्षोणीरुहान् हर्षयन्
शैलान् विद्रवयन् मृगान् विवशयन् गोवृन्दमानन्दयन् ।
गोपान् संभ्रमयन् मुनीन् मुकुलयन् सप्तस्वरान् जृंभयन्
ओंकारार्थमुदीरयन् विजयते वंशीनिनादः शिशोः ॥

**Hearing the melodies arising from the flute of child
Krishna, the worlds become enraptured
The Vedas turn melodious, trees bloom,
mountains shine
Animals find energy, cows are happy,
and cowboys joyous
Sages turn meditative as the musical notes reach a
crescendo and echoes of Om reverberate in the universe**

I am Baashi.

I look simple but I am intricate and demanding.

I call for diligence, for a method and appropriate
measures failing which I cannot deliver melody. The

positioning of the finger holes is calculated by measuring the bamboo shaft's inner and outer diameters.

There is a formula in creating me. It is a special skill and this has to be intuitive, it cannot be taught or mentored.

The biggest challenge in structuring me is that I don't give my creator a second chance. The flute maker has only one chance to burn my holes and a single mistake in calculation will ruin me forever. He knows this and is careful to initiate a small hole, he then plays the note using a chromatic tuner and a drone called tanpura and gradually, bit by bit, with focused trial and adjustments, he invents a melody by sanding the holes in small increments.

The process of my formation is long and arduous. I am demanding of patience, of passion.

After all the holes are perfected on my body, I am steeped in a solution of antiseptic oils, then I am cleaned, dried and my ends are bound with silk or nylon threads for both, decoration as well as protection against thermal expansion.

It is unfortunate that while so much is known and written about me, very little is known about the flute maker, without whom I have no existence.

I am feelings.

Created with feelings.

Played with feelings.

I am easy to hurt and easy to break.

My Lord Krishna knew this and preserved me, wrapped in silk and tucked in his waistband, and protected from sun and rain. He knew I was cold in the winter, that I expanded unevenly and often cracked, unable to bear the wind and so, always wrapped me in his shawl.

He knew I am fragile and guarded me in diverse climate, oiled me in the night to keep me strong and sturdy. I have memories of the warm mustard oil served by Yashoda maa at night, tenderly massaged by my Lord before he rested me to sleep beside him.

Sometimes, Kaanha's sakhas wanted to pamper me and soaked me in linseed and walnut oil but they were not as well versed in the delicate process as my Lord, and this often had adverse effects. They were unaware that my threads and the blowing hole had to remain dry and in their ignorance, caused me harm. My Lord was worried because after that I lost my voice for a few days.

Kaanha spent all his time nursing me with an oil soaked cotton swab. He gently applied the oil on my inside, and few inches away from the blowing hole. He let me soak in the fragrance and rest till completely dry and ready for another melody, on another day.

Not everyone can figure me out but those who do travel with me, stay with me a lifetime.

In the olden days, I was played with six-finger holes but over the years, the emerging maestros experimented with an additional seventh hole which enables them to play a half step lower than on a six-hole flute and with the seventh hole closed, I serve as low as Teevra Maa which is extremely useful in raagas like Raag Yaman and Raag Puriya.

I am melody.
I am bansi.
I am tradition.
I am bansuri.
I am ancient.
I am Murli.
I am Keshava's beloved.

गोपालाजिरकर्दमे विहरसे विप्राध्वरे लज्जसे
ब्रूषे गोकुलहुंकृतैः स्तुतिशतैर्मौनं विधत्से विदाम् ।
दास्यं गोकुलपुंश्चलीषु कुरुषे स्वाम्यं न दान्तात्मसु
ज्ञातं कृष्ण! तवाङ्घ्रियुगलं प्रेम्णा चलं मज्जलम् ॥

O Krishna! You play in the muddy
courtyards of cowherd boys
But you shy away from the sacrifice of brahmanas;
You respond to the "hum" calls of cows
But you are silent when you are praised by
hundreds of hymns by wise men;
You do the bidding of women of easy virtue in gokula
But you do not want to be Lord of those
who have controlled their senses
I know why it is so; your pretty lotus-like feet are
moved only by love and devotion

नमस्तस्मै यशोदाया
दायादायाऽस्तु तेजसे ।
यद्धि रधामुखांभोजं
भोजं भोजं व्यववर्धत ॥

Salutations to that effulgence who is the son of Yashoda
And who grew up always enjoying watching
the lotus face of Radha

अवतारा सन्त्वन्ये
सरसिजनयनस्य सर्वतोभद्राः ।
कृष्णादन्यः को वा
प्रभवति गोगोपगोपिकामुक्त्यै ॥

There may be many other incarnations of
the lotus-eyed Vishnu
Which are auspicious in every way
But, except Krishna
Who else is capable of liberating the cows?
Cowherd men and cowherd women?

Kadamba Tree

The Kadamba Tree is symbolic of romance because it was
beneath the Kadamba Tree in Vrindavan that Radha
and Kaanha spent time together.

Kadamba

I AM TALL AND ORNAMENTAL

अयि जगदम्ब मदम्ब कदम्ब वनप्रियवासिनि हासरते
शिखरि शिरोमणि तुझ्हिमलय शृझ्निजालय मध्यगते ।
मधुमधुरे मधुकैटभगञ्जिनि कैटभभञ्जिनि रासरते
जय जय हे महिषासुरमर्दिनि रम्यकपर्दिनि शैलसुते ॥

Salutations to the Mother of the Universe
Who is my own mother and likes to live in the
forest of Kadamba Trees
She delights in laughter and mirth and
dwells in the lofty Himalayas
She is as sweet as honey and destroyed
demons like Madhu and Kaitabha
Victory to you, the destroyer of demon Mahishasura
You have beautiful locks of hair and are the
daughter of the mountain

I am Kadamba.

I grow in many continents but in India I am predominantly associated with Vrindavan, the land of Radha Rani and Lord Krishna, who was then just Kaanha of Gokul.

I am Lord Krishna and Radha Rani's confidante.

It was beneath my shade and the veil of my orange leaves that love blossomed between the two and turned legendary.

The world knows about their undying love but I know so much more which I will never share.

Not surprising then that I am described as precious and ornamental. My beautiful ochre leaves and my scented flowers have manifold stories to tell. Stories of romance, stories of intrigue.

The seers say that Lord Krishna chose me as his rendezvous because of my purity and aesthetics. I believe that it was the presence of Radha Rani and my Lord around me that spreads fragrance. My bark shone and my leaves spread each time they touched me.

The orchard and the forest blossomed every time they walked the path hand in hand and when they dispersed, my leaves wilted and withered away.

I am tall and luscious; I grow fast and transform colour according to seasons.

Sometimes I feel I am symbolic of Radha Rani's volatile moods. I reflect her fire and her passion. She blushes pink when Kaanha is beside her, when he touches her and turns green with envy when he shifts attention to the gopikas. She is red-eyed when furious and ash-faced when it came to parting with her beloved.

They spend long, silent hours seated beneath my foliage resembling a canopy. I have guarded them from atop and my long branches coiled together have gently rocked them to sleep.

Moments of utter bliss.

When Kaanha played the flute and Radha Rani laid her head on his shoulder, lost in sweet dreams, their love was palpable and visible to all of Vrindavan—the gwalas, gopikas, the birds, and the animals.

We all believed that their love will last forever and ever. We didn't know then that love comes with a price and like all true lovers of the universe, Radha Rani and Kaanha had to part ways and lead separate lives. I guess there is no escaping the call of the cosmos, is this what they call destiny?

Every parting is painful and who understands this better than a tree? If I had my way, I would preserve my every branch, every leaf, and every fruit but that was not to be. From time to time I have had to watch all my fruit fall and leaves blown away by the rain, uncaring of my longing for them.

Radha Rani and Kaanha separated when he left for Mathura and I was a witness of their suffering.

I remember that afternoon when Kaanha was set to leave with brother Balarama. I remember his last meeting with Radha Rani beneath my branches. He was weary and Radha Rani, heavy-hearted. She cried and embraced him again and again. He stroked her gently pacifying her again and again but she was inconsolable and pleaded with Kaanha to not leave Gokul, to not leave her.

My branches soaked in her tears and grief and my leaves

trembled in her longing for Kaanha. That evening the sky suddenly turned gloomy and the forest looked desolate as if something untoward was to happen.

It did. Kaanha left Gokula forever.

That was the last time he visited me, the last time he touched me. He bid goodbye silently, dispassionately, and when he finally walked out of the forest, he did not look back.

That evening Radha Rani was not the only one who was heartbroken. All the trees in the forest, all the birds and the bees were in despair.

I am Kadamba.

I preserve secrets of loved ones.

I am Indicus.

I am blessed to have been touched by the deities.

Kustitanga

I AM EDIBLE AND ALSO MEDICINAL

The Kadamba is also identified as the tree with shade
and therefore visible on roadsides, avenues, and villages.

गौरीं काञ्चनपद्मिनीतटगृहां श्रीसुन्दरेशप्रियां
नीपारण्यसुवर्णकन्दकपरिक्रीडाविलोलामुमाम् ।
श्रीमद्पाण्ड्यकुलाचलाग्रविलसद्रत्नप्रदीपायितां
मीनाक्षीं मधुरेश्वरीं शुकधरां श्रीपाण्ड्यबालांभजे ॥

Salutations to Meenakshi, who is goddess of Madurai
Who has a bird in her hand, who is the
daughter of Pandya king
Who is Gowri, who has a temple near the
golden lotus tank
Who is the darling of Lord Sundareswara
Who is the goddess Uma, who likes to play with
the golden ball
In the forest of Kadamba trees
And who is the gem-studded lamp lit on the top
of the peak of Pandya clan

When Kaanha deserted Gokul, I turned forlorn and I shudder to think of what Radha Rani went through in his absence.

She stopped visiting the forest. I missed their presence sorely. I was accustomed to their daily chatter and I felt incomplete without them.

Kaanha never said it in so many words but I knew I was his friend and confidante. We were sakhas and it did not matter who between the two of us is older.

The old guards say I was discovered in the year 1785 in a remote place called Madagascar but unsure of my origin, they were unable to give me a name.

Others say that in the year 1830, a learned man called Achille Richard named me Anthocephalus because he researched that I originated in Asia but it was a complicated name and therefore not easily acceptable.

So many stories just over just my origin, just like my sakha. After so many years, we are still intrigued about Kaanha's miracle birth and escape from Dwarka on a dark, stormy night.

We are intrigued by stories of his childhood pranks, his foster parents' obsession with him, we are enchanted by his adventures and enamoured by his sublime romance with Radha Rani and their tragic separation.

It has been so many years but we still reinterpret and redefine everything associated with him.

Technology has altered lifestyles but even today, many of us preserve his butter pot just like the ancient times in our home kitchens, his flute and conch reside in our temples, and his peacock feather decorates his statue. We pass by a Kadamba tree and pause momentarily to ponder over his truants with the gopikas in Vrindavan.

Sri Krishna loved trees and all the trees loved him but I would like to believe that I am Kaanha's favourite tree.

He has climbed on my branches and pelted stones to break so many butter pots of so many milkmaids. He has rested on my bark, playing the flute on so many afternoons and when he grew older, romanced Radha Rani beneath my shade.

Therefore when he left for Dwarka, it was not just Radha Rani but all of Gokula and Vrindavan that turned desolate.

My green/orange branches turned yellow in longing for Kaanha and my bark withered away unable to watch a lonesome Radha Rani weeping inconsolably, hiding behind my tree. Radha Rani yearned for Kaanha and I yearned for them to be together.

Those were bleak days.

I worried for Radha Rani and feared that she would never be the same again. I was right. She withdrew from life, never visited me, her favourite Kadamba and her Kaanha's sakha.

I longed for her presence in my forest but the dry leaves never heard her anklets again.

My heart was heavy for a long time and was sure I would never bloom again, never bear fruit again. I was wrong.

I survived because I was born to endure, to spread

fragrance and the coming generations discovered the useful side to me.

I never told them my story, never told them how Kaanha and Radha Rani plucked my fruits and relished them.

In the coming years, the scientists discovered that my leaves are edible for cattle. I did not tell them that Kaanha's wish-fulfilling cow Kamadhenu had all along fed on my leaves and slept peacefully while his master played the flute. I am Lamarckia.

In present times my utility is manifold. I am exploited for timber and paper, for plywood, for light construction, for pulp, for boxes and crates, for dug-out canoes, and for furniture components. I am also used to create perfume and my leaves serve as a mouth wash.

My bark is bitter so purposeful in inflammatory diseases, gastropathy, cough, vomitting, ulcers, and debility. A decoction of my leaves cures ulcers and metrorrhagia. My fruits cure gastric irritability and fever.

Many preserve my fallen leaves as a book mark and some use them for decomposition. I improve the physical and chemical properties of soil under its canopy.

I am Kadamba.

I preserve secrets and also nature.

~ IV.3 ~

Katambu

I AM AUSPICIOUS; I AM FERTILE

The Kadamba tree is said to represent Shatabhisha/Aquarii
and has a special place in mythology.

जटाभुजङ्गपिङ्गलस्फुरत्फणामणिप्रभा
कदम्बकुङ्कुमद्रवप्रलिप्तदिग्वधूमुखे ।
मदान्धसिन्धुरस्फुरत्त्वगुत्तरीयमेदुरे
मनो विनोदमद्भुतं बिभर्तु भूतभर्तरि ॥

May my mind hold Shiva with the light from
the jewels of his shining hood
Of creeper-like yellow snakes
The face of Dikkanyas smeared with Kadamba
juice like red Kuṅkuma
That looks dense due to the glittering skin garment
of the intoxicated Elephant
And who is the Lord of the ghosts

I am Karam.

I am mentioned in the Bhagavata Purana.

While every tree associated with Lord Krishna is precious
and documented as some art form, I am fortunate that poets

like Jaydeva's Geet Govinda have dedicated verses to me. I am fortunate that many performing artistess have paid tributes in immortal images to me.

In North India, I am synonymous with Lord Krishna, some address me as my Lord's sakha, while others describe me as his avatar.

Down South I am referred to as the Parvati's tree and in some regions as Rohini's tree. While the Radha-Krishna romance beneath Kadamba is legendary, it is believed that in the Sangam period of Tamil Nadu, Murugan of Tirupparankundram Hill of Madurai was referred to as a centre of nature worship because Murugan in the form of a spear is placed under me, a Kadamba tree.

So many stories, so many interpretations.

We are all familiar with Lord Krishna as a naughty, young boy, eve-teasing the gopikas bathing at the pond. The story is portrayed in so many paintings and dance forms, Shabdam in Bharatanatyam specifically is dedicated to performing Krishna robbing the costumes and then sitting on top of a tree and playing his bansuri.

This story apparently has a deeper message that most of us have missed out.

It is said that the sea-god Lord Varuna, had forbidden nude bathing inside the rivers, the ponds, and other public places, but the carefree gopikas never adhered to the rule and it was to teach them a lesson, that Lord Krishna one day, reached the bank of the pond and stole their garments and spread them on the branches of a nearby Kadamba tree.

He refused to return the garments to the gopikas till they pleaded and apologised for their mistake. The dance form where gopikas apologise is more spiritual than physical. They seek forgiveness from Lord Varuna for disobeying his orders.

I know this because I was present that time and witnessed the drama; I witnessed the trauma of the gopikas on not finding their garments. I understood the significance because my Lord interpreted it for me. He wanted me to understand the relevance so that I would remember and recount the story in different lifetimes to different generations.

I am Kadamba.

I am privileged to have witnessed that era, privileged that history walked me through so many milestones.

Very few know that a dynasty is named after me—Banavasi is now the state of Karnataka from 345 CE to 525 CE as per Talagunda inscription of c.450 where I am revered and offered prayers like an ancestor even today.

Very few know that I am also associated with the tree deity—Kadambariyamman—Kadamba, considered the sthalavruksham or the tree of the place and also known as Kadambavana. I am omnipresent inside Meenakshi Amman temple and worshipped in the harvest festival popularly known as Karam-Kadamba.

This is celebrated on the eleventh lunar day of the month Bhadarva in India and in many regions, the ceremony includes a twig of the tree brought home by the lady of the house and revered in the courtyard of the home.

Later in the day, the grain is distributed among friends, neighbours and relatives. This festive custom has been adopted by the Tulu community in Andhra Pradesh and popularised by different names in neighbouring regions for instance Onam in Kerala and Huttari in Kodagu, but all are described as Kadambotsava, meaning the festival of Kadamba.

Our scriptures profess that the twenty-seven nakshatras, constituting twelve Houses or Rasis and nine planets, are specifically represented precisely by twenty-seven trees—one for each star. The Kadamba tree is said to represent Shatabhisha which is why you will often find me outside temples and identify me by my red and orange colour flowers that, in full bloom, take the shape of a ball.

I have a special place in mythology and I am the favourite of not just Lord Krishna and Lord Murugan, both avatars of Lord Vishnu, but also a favourite of all the deities, and therefore addressed as Haripriya, meaning the God's favourite.

Mother Goddess Durga adores me and one of the reasons for this is that I am considered fertile. May be that is why she resides inside a Kadamba forest and maybe that is also the reason I am considered suitable for reforestation programs.

I am Shatabhisha.

I am Attutekku.

The natives believe that planting me in close proximity to lakes and ponds, ushers in happiness and prosperity in life.

I am Neolamarckia.

I am auspicious.

हे गोपालक हे कृपाजलनिधे हे सिन्धुकन्यापते
हे कंसान्तक हे गजेन्द्रकरुणापारीण हे माधव ।
हे रामानुज हे जगत्त्रयगुरो हे पुण्डरीकाक्ष मां
हे गोपीजननाथ पालय परं जानामि न त्वां विना ॥

O protector of cows! O ocean of mercy!
O consort of Lakshmi! O slayer of Kamsa!
O merciful saviour of Gajendra! Madhava!
O Younger brother of Balarama!
O teacher of the three worlds!
O Lotus-eyed one, save me, protect me, I do not
know any God higher than you

कस्तूरीतिलकं ललाटफलके वक्षःस्थले कौस्तुभं
नासाग्रे नवमौक्तिकं करतले वेणुं करे कङ्कणम् ।
सर्वाङ्गे हरिचन्दनं च कलयन् कण्ठे च मुक्तावलिं
गोपस्त्री परिवेष्टितो विजयते गोपालचूडामणिः ॥

Victory to the crest jewel of cowherds
Who sports a tilak of kasturi on the forehead and
Kaustubha jewel on his chest
Who wears a nose-ring of pearls and who carries
a flute in his hand

Who wears bracelets on his wrists; he has smeared
sandalwood paste all over his body
Who wears a chain of pearls around the neck and
who is surrounded on all sides by the gopis

यस्यात्मभूतस्य गुरोः प्रसादा-
दहं विमुक्तोऽस्मि शरीरबन्धात् ।
सर्वोपदेष्टु पुरुषोत्तमस्य
तस्याङ्घ्रिपद्मं प्रणतोऽस्मि नित्यम् ॥

I prostrate before the lotus feet of that guru, the best
among men and advisor of everything to be known
The very self in me and by the blessings of whom
I was released from the bonds of this body.

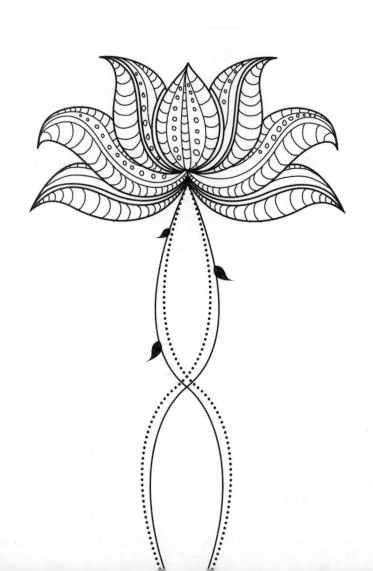

CHAPTER V

Kamala

Some say the lotus flower came to be associated with Krishna
after he became Dwarkadhish but folklore and ancient
paintings reveal that Kaanha always loved the Kamala and
used it as a metaphor to impart his teachings.

Kamala

I RISE IN THE WATER

One who performs his duty without attachment,
surrendering the results unto the Supreme Lord, is
unaffected by sinful action, as the lotus is untouched
by water—Bhagavad Gita

ब्रह्मण्याधाय कर्माणि सङ्गं त्यक्त्वा करोति य: ।
लिप्यते न स पापेन पद्मपत्रमिवाम्भसा ॥

The person who performs actions
Offers them to brahmana, the Supreme
Abandons attachment and is not tainted
by sin Just as a lotus leaf
That remains unaffected by the water on it

I am Kamala.

Some call me Sacred Water Lily; some call me Bean of
India but most know me as Kamala. I rise in the water and I
am recognised by my broad floating leaves and my
characteristic fragrance.

I stand on long and firm stems and my many petals
overlap each other in a symmetrical pattern.

My roots are deep and spread out through the muddy soil of the pond or river bottom. My large circular leaves often dressed in dew drops float on top of the water surface.

I have many names, many references and all of them have myriad interpretations.

In India I am called Ambal, Thamarai, Suriya Kamal, Padma, Ambuja, and Pankaja.

I grow in different shapes and sizes in different seasons, and different countries refer to me by different titles.

In America I am smaller in size and paler in colour and they call me Nelumbium Luteum.

In China I am usually pink and sometimes white and they call me Nelumbium Nelumbo.

In Egypt, like in India, I am associated with mythology. I am revered as the mother of the sun and this is because I bloom by day and wilt by the night.

I am Ambala.

I have many colours.

When I am white I am described as Pundarika...I symbolise spiritual perfection and mental purity and this comes from the celestial stars. My petals spread and absorb the natural beauty of the shining stars in the sky.

When I am pink I am addressed as Padma... the supreme lotus reserved for the highest deity.

When I am red I am referred to as Kamala... it signifies purity of the heart. Then, I am the lotus of love, of passion, the flower of Avalokiteshvara, the bodhisattva of compassion.

When I am blue I am called Utpala...I am a symbol of victory of spirit over senses, symbol of wisdom of knowledge and the flower of Manjushri, the bodhisattva of wisdom.

My seeds, not always visible, are hard and dark in colour and alter in shape from round to oval to oblong. I blossom in the mornings but when the sun rises my petals feel weary and fall off.

Artists and poets have, for generations, paid tribute to my beauty. It is either the Lotus-eyed or the Lotus feet and both have traditional significance. The Lotus-eyed is symbolic for Lord Krishna and the Lotus feet, an expression of submission to both the deity and also to the guru.

I am Thamarai.

I rise from unclean water and remain uncontaminated.

I am the flower of the deities and therefore sacred.

I represent the divine birth and also the creation.

Padmaja

I AM RESURRECTION

In the citadel of the body, there is the small sinless and
pure lotus of the heart which is the residence of the
Supreme Mahanarayana Upanishad.

श्रुतीनां मूर्धानो दधति तव यौ शेखरतया
ममाप्येतौ मातः शिरसि दयया देहि चरणौ ।
ययोः पाद्यं पाथः पशुपति जटाजूट तटिनी
ययोः लाक्षा लक्ष्मीः अरुण हरिचूडामणि रुचिः ॥

Soundarya Lahari 84

O my Mother Sridevi!
The Holy Vedas
Hold your lotus feet
As ornaments on their heads
Place your feet on my head
The water that washes your lotus feet
Is the river Ganga flowing over the
matted hair of Lord Shiva?
Your lotus feet are adorned with red lac, with the
red lustre from Lord Vishnu's crest jewel

I am Surya Kamal.

The seers say my birth is for a reason, to impart a message. I emerge from the muddy water and blossom into a flower. The human being also, on its path to enlightenment fades away impurities before coming into soul consciousness.

I symbolise resurrection.

I break away from my entangled weeds and float above water without a trace of mud, so does the balance of life.

I am the flower of the golden age, associated with Lord Krishna and other deities always holding my stem in their hand. If not in their hand I am always found placed at the feet of the deities.

Lord Ganesha and Goddess Lakshmi are always depicted standing or seated atop me. Lord Brahma, the god of creation is depicted as emerging from a lotus that crawls from the navel of Lord Vishnu.

I am symbolic of their quality of life, pure and wholesome.

I am symbolic of detachment, of life devoid of expectations and finally, symbolic of togetherness.

I am Padma.

I am never alone in the pond. There are always other lotuses, layers of mud, leaves, water, sunlight, and dew drops around me.

I give the impression of being alone but I am always in the company of nature.

Lord Krishna is never in isolation. He is always surrounded by his cowherd friends or the sensuous milkmaids; he is surrounded by cattle, the birds, his family, and very often the entire village, a characteristic of the golden age where nobody is sad or lonely and every day and night is a celebration.

The deities symbolise contentment and their presence exudes a fragrance, which is why they are referred to as kanchan kaya, which means a body devoid of disease.

In Vedic scripture, the body of Lord Krishna, an incarnation of Lord Vishnu, is described as a bluish new-grown lotus flower and it represents beauty and non-attachment.

I am Ambuja.

I represent the sacred place, the heart and my unfolding petals are an expansion of my soul.

I am a symbol of bhakti or love for God or Paramatma or the super soul who resides in our heart.

I am privileged that the holy Ganga is strewn with my petals, overwhelmed that I am the chosen one to be offered in devotion. There are stories within stories and all of them have a precious message.

The unopened Lotus bud is representative of a folded soul that has the ability to uplift and elevate above the muddy surroundings and aspire for the divine truth.

My ancestors symbolised the ten prime virtues requisite in worship to the Lord, namely: purity, beauty, majesty, grace, fertility, wealth, richness, knowledge, serenity, and eternity and the tradition continues after all these years.

I do not grow in Tibet yet I feature among the eight auspicious symbols of their country.

If you notice the standing Buddha idols you will always find them resting on a separate lotus.

I bloom and spread cheer, I spread fragrance.

When I am plucked from the weed I am offered to the deity.

When I wilt away, I become medicine.

I am Kamala.

Being at the feet of the deities for so many eons I have learned that receiving is in giving.

When Lord Krishna's gurukul friend, Sudama carried a handful of rice for his friend and queen Rukmini, my Lord gave him manifold in return.

I have internalised that and lived by the philosophy.

 V.3

Aravinda

I AM HERBAL

Oh, Human! This life of yours is balanced on the lotus leaf and your lifespan is just like a drop of water running down that leaf, which may fall any minute—Vedas

त्रयाणां देवानां त्रिगुणजनितानां तव शिवे
भवेत्पूजा पूजा तव चरणयोर्या विरचिता ।

तथाहि त्वत्पादोद्वहन मणिपीठस्य निकटे
स्थिता ह्येते शश्वन्मुकुलितकरोत्तंस मकुटाः ॥

Soundarya Lahari 25

**O! auspicious Parashakti
When your sacred feet are worshipped, that becomes
equal to venerating the three Gods, Brahma, Vishnu
and Shiva, the embodiments of your three guṇas, who
always stand close to your gem decked foot pedestal,
holding their hands above their heads.**

I am Ambuja.

Everyone knows I am fragrant but few are aware that I can heal and cure, too.

Ayurveda experts profess that my seeds are classified as astringent and benefits the human kidney, spleen, and heart. The astringent also comes in use when there is loss of kidney function.

My seeds help rejuvenate weak libidos in men and leucorrhoea in women.

Inside the seed is the green embryo that benefits the human heart.

My seeds also cure restlessness, palpitation, and insomnia.

My beautiful circular leaves are prescribed as an antidote for mushroom poisoning. They also cure heart and liver disorders.

My leaves in combination with the other herbs treat sunstroke, dysentery, fever, and vomiting of blood.

Portions of me are also used in traditional Asian herbal medicine.

I am Aravinda.

I am a flower, herbal plant and edible, too.

My fruit is a conical pod—Nucifera indicates a hard fruit. When the seeds are ripe, they become loose in the pod. The pod then tips down towards the water and gradually releases the seeds.

When my petals drop off they are replaced by a flat-topped seed pod divided into compartments that resemble a wasp's hive. The tender seeds beneath it are habitually munched in north-east India.

I am Kamala.

I am useful in the kitchen as well. My seeds, Phool Makhana are popular in Indian cuisine.

Some ancient families dry and store me for longer use like pickles.

My leaves and stalk are eaten as vegetable in many regions in India.

My tubers taste like sweet potato.

My petals are used for garnish and my fan like leaves serve as wraps for fillings.

My seeds, my leaves, and rhizomes are all edible.

My stem is eaten in all parts of India, and pickled too.

I am Saroja.

Pankaja

I AM THE SYMBOL OF LOVE AND RECTITUDE

According to legend, Gautama Buddha was
born with the ability to walk, and lotus flowers
bloomed everywhere he stepped.

हिमानी हन्तव्यं हिमगिरिनिवासैक चतुरौ
निशायां निद्राणं निशि चरमभागे च विशदौ ।
वरं लक्ष्मीपात्रं श्रिय-मतिसृजन्तौ समयिनां
सरोजं त्वत्पादौ जननि जयतश्चित्रमिह किम् ॥

Soundarya Lahari *87*

Lotus blights in snowfall
Your lotus feet
Dwell in snow-clad mountains
Sleep during the night
Shine both at night and day
Bestowing Sri Lakshmi to her devotees
Between a lotus and your lotus feet
O Mother Sridevi

I am Saroja.

I am the symbol of love because unlike other flowers, I never break completely.

When I wilt I separate into two parts but remain connected with fibres and roots which is why I am used as a metaphor for lovers when describing everlasting romance.

I am the symbol of rectitude.

I am sacred and incorruptible.

I am the symbol of triumph.

I am divine, I am fertile.

I am wealth and I am knowledge.

I am one of the eight auspicious symbols of Indian classical art.

The Purnakalasa symbolises abundance and creativity and depicts overflowing foliage comprising lotus buds, lotus flowers, and lotus leaves. The motifs of Purankalasa are found in our heritages, the legendary Taj Mahal in Agra, which some believe to be an ancient Hindu Temple rebuilt by the Muslims, where I am the prominent motif.

I am Suvarna Kamala.

I occupy a special position in the art of ancient India, both written and oral literature of the country.

I am rooted in the mud and survive calamities; I symbolise longevity, honour and fortune.

I am offered in prayers, so linked to religion.

Puranic Vedas and mythology quote me as a sacred flower.

The artists and the poets have always been fascinated

with my form, featured me in their songs as an allegory for singing odes to feminine beauty. "Hang my head and touch the lotus, it is as clear as water" says a poet to present his purity of love. Another poet describes the beauty of his beloved as "lotus like face."

Sculptors and painters have sustained my glory with new names, such as Neeraja, Pankaja, Kamala and Saroja.

I am Nalin.

I am a water plant but unattained by muddy water surroundings.

There are many water plants but I am the only one with the ability to stay afloat because I have a strong stem that holds me eight to twelve inches above the water surface.

It is for these characteristics that I am chosen as the national flower of India.

I am also the national flower of Vietnam.

I am revered as a deity in Egypt because they regard me as the symbol of the Sun God.

In China I am a symbol of harmony and immortalised in folk art with images of fairies holding me in their hands.

I am Nalini.

I am lotus.

I am the flower of worship, of the artistes, of the deities.

There is a beautiful chant associated with me, and it goes like this.

रात्रिर्गमिष्यति भविष्यति सुप्रभातं
भानुरुदेश्यति हसिष्यति कमल श्री: ।
इत्थं विचारयति कोषगते द्विरेफे
हा! हन्त! हन्त! नलिनीं गज उज्जहार ॥

Night will fade
There will be morning
The sun will rise
The lotus flower will bloom
as the bee inside the flower thought
so the lotus
Was uprooted by an elephant

मध्येगोकुलमण्डलं प्रतिदिशं चांबारवोज्जृंभिते
प्रातर्दोहमहोत्सवे नवघनश्यामं रणन्नूपुरम् ।
फाले बालविभूषणं कटिरटत्सकिङ्किणीमेखलं
कण्ठे व्याघ्रनखञ्च शैशवकलाकल्याणकास्मर्यं भजे ॥

I pray to Krishna, the very acme of beauty
And auspiciousness of childhood
In the midst of the early morning festivity
of milking the cows
That fills the air with their "Ambaa" cry
There is child Krishna, dark blue as the
newly formed cloud
Anklets tinkling, forehead adorned by a tilak
The small bells in the hip belt tinkling
And wearing a tiger-nail ornament around his neck

सजलजलदनीलं दर्शितोदारलीलं
करतलधृतशैलं वेणुनादेरसालम् ।
व्रजजनकुलपालं कामिनीकेलिलोलं
कलितललितमालं नौमि गोपालबालम् ॥

I salute that child Gopala, who is dark blue
as the water-bearing clouds
Whose playful acts are generous, who lifted up
and held a mountain with one hand
Who enjoys the music of the flute and takes
care of the people of Vraja
Who is fond of playing with the belles of Vraja and
who wears a beautiful garland of wild flowers

स्मितललितकपोलं स्निग्धसंगीतलोलं
ललितचिकुरजालं चौर्यचातुर्यलीलम् ।
शतमखरिपुकालं शातकुम्भाभचेलं
कुवलयदलनीलं नौमि गोपालबालम् ॥

Child Gopala with
chubby cheeks lit by a beautiful smile
Who enjoys sweet music and has beautiful locks of hair
Who is clever in his playful stealing, who is Death
to the enemies of Indra
And who is of dark blue complexion as the
petals of the blue lily

CHAPTER VI

Tulsi

Tulsi plant, associated with Lord Vishnu, is the
centre of Vaishnavite worship, the manifestation of
God in the plant world.

Tulsi-Mata

I AM DIVINITY

The divine Tulsi is incomparable.
One that gives pleasure to the Gods: Devadundubhi

नमस्तुलसी कल्याणी नमो विष्णुप्रिये शुभे ।
नमो मोक्षप्रदे देवी नमः सम्पत्प्रदायिनी ॥

**Salutations to you, Oh Goddess Tulsi
The provider of fruits of all wishes
Salutations to you, who are adorable
for the three worlds
Salutations to you, who protects the world**

Simply by seeing
Simply by touching
Simply by remembering
Simply by praying to
Simply by bowing before
Simply by hearing about
Or simply by sowing me
…there is auspiciousness.

My devotees swear by my powerful presence. They have heard about what transpired in the Heavens several centuries ago.

One day, when Lord Krishna's youngest queen Satyabhama decided to weigh her husband in gold, all her wealth and ornaments could not tilt the scale. But then his older queen Rukmini Devi arrived with a plateful of my leaves. Older and wiser, she placed just a single leaf on the pan and the scale tilted—much to Satyabhama's astonishment!

Satyabhama questioned how could I be so precious and Rukmini Devi answered, "Because Lord Krishna so desired."

It is my Lord's blessings that I am revered and every part of my being has a reason and a mission. My root, like every other plant, is for procreation but it is also symbolic for all the sacred places of pilgrimage. The centre of my stem is the dwelling place of all the deities and my upper branches are sacrosanct, for in them are embodied all the Vedas.

It was His vardaan that everything about me—my leaves, twigs, flowers, buds including the soil in which I grow— possesses spiritual power.

It was His desire that I am a manifestation of the Goddess and, therefore, it is my destiny to endure such a varied and a colourful past!

It is a story everybody knows but I will recount it for those who do not. Lord Vishnu spawned me from the Samudramanthana, the churning of the cosmic ocean, as a vital aid for all mankind and for the spiritual upliftment of human souls in the material world. I didn't know it then, but in the coming time I would have to assume many roles.

Sometimes I am the fourth incarnation of the Goddess appearing at the beginning of our present age, the Kalyug, to whom prayers are offered morning and evening by men and women in every household.

Sometimes I am Vrinda tricked into seduction by Lord Vishnu leading to the demise of my husband Jalandhara. So enraged was I by his deception that I cursed Lord Vishnu and transformed Him into the Shaligrama stone. He did but not before getting even with me. He retaliated by turning me into a Tulsi plant.

It was Lord Vishnu's benevolence that rendered me sacred on earth. In my avatar as Lakshmi, I once quarrelled bitterly with Goddess Saraswati and her curse transformed me into a Tulsi plant, forcing me to henceforth live my life on earth forever. But when I was reunited with Lord Vishnu, I was overjoyed, and so was my friend river Gandaki which, in ecstasy, flowed from my body in the shape of the Holy Tulsi plant.

Sometimes I am worshipped as a mother. They address me as Tulsi-mata. I symbolise the perfect householder who assures domestic bliss. Hindus revere me for my holiness. It is because the Lord averred that among plants, He was Tulsi. So along with river Yamuna and mountain Govardhan, I am omnipresent in the spiritual world.

It is my honour to occupy space at my Lord's feet, my privilege to adorn his neck with a garland of leaves.

He may never say it to me in so many words but I know that I am very, very dear to my Lord…perhaps more than even Goddess Lakshmi.

He is aware of my extreme austerities to attain him as my husband. Sometimes I sense that Goddess Lakshmi is disapproving of my unwavering presence at my Lord's feet. I understand; after all she is the Goddess of Fortune while I am just a plant, but a plant without which the Lord will not accept any offerings.

My attachment to my Lord culminates in a moment of ecstasy on the eleventh bright day of the month of Kartika when Lord Vishnu, the Protector, the Preserver, and one among the Trimurti along with Lord Brahma, the Creator and Shiva, the Destroyer, concedes to marry me.

I am Haripriya.

Perhaps it is a combination of all these virtues and my undying devotion to my Lord that I have become the central symbol of the Vaishnavites. Widows worship me for salvation, un-married girls to obtain good husbands, married couples for children, and the elderly for attaining a place in paradise.

Few people are aware of this but I contain Shiva's semen in my stem and therefore I am precious to the Shaivites as well.

I have multiple avatars. Lord Vishnu devotees perceive me as Lakshmi or Vrinda; Krishna bhaktas revere me as Radha or Rukmini while devotees of Rama view in me the image of Sita.

As Vrinda, you will find me in temples like Tulsi Manas Mandir in Varanasi and, of course, Vrindavan. It was in Vrindavan that Radha Rani and Lord Krishna fell in love with each other and I fell in love with Lord Krishna.

Our old customs emphasise that there is no better recipient of charity than the poor and needy, no better gift than cattle, no better pilgrimage than the Ganges, and no better leaf than mine.

The courtyard is my abode and the Ashtadhalam or the eight-petalled lotus holding me, my quintessential identity. The lady of the house where I reside wakes me up at dawn with a pot of water and later at twilight lights a lamp to invoke Goddess Lakshmi within me for prosperity.

I am a purifier.

Offer me obeisance and I will vanquish lifetimes of sins. Place me in your home and I will transform it into a place of pilgrimage devoid of disease and death. Wherever the wind carries my aroma, I will purify the atmosphere and free up animals from all their baser tendencies. My Lord Vishnu will follow me to all the homes where I am cultivated and nourished.

I am protection.

Lord Krishna and Lord Hanuman, though courageous, wear garlands of me. My single leaf is more precious than an offering of jewels, and pearls. When a devotee offers me at the feet of my Lord, he is released of sins accumulated over lifetimes. When a devotee offers me to the head of my Lord, he is freed of unforeseen sins and calamities.

I am salvation.

God resides wherever I am worshipped. Walk around me and all karmic blockages will be cleared. Water me and gain blessings of religious acts. Wear me as a necklace and discard your fears.

I am contribution.

Every part of me—my roots, leaves, seeds, and bark—contribute in the last rites of a human. A person who is cremated with a Tulsi twig in his mouth attains moksh regardless of his sins.

I am devotion.

One who applies my paste to the deity of Lord Krishna will reside close to the Lord. One who smears the mud from the base of my tree on his body reaps the result of a hundred days of devotion each day. One who spreads my glories to others will never take birth again.

I am righteousness.

As Kalyani, my leaves and roots are a cure for several diseases. As Vishnupriya, I safeguard the health of humans and animals. As Moksaprade, I help to keep the mind healthy and free for spiritual pursuits.

I am Divinity.

I am incomparable.

I am Tulsi.

There are special prayers devoted to me in the Padma Purana. It says

"Oh supreme Tulsi, the best Gods sing your glory. Even sages, siddhas and the Lord of the snakes do not fully comprehend your glories...the measures of your qualities after hundreds of crores of kalpas. You emerged from the joy of Vishnu at the time of the churning of the milk ocean."

Since Vishnu held me on his head, since I touched the limbs of the Almighty it is believed that I will be able to dissolve obstacles in their path and reach them to the highest position.

Legend has it that I was planted on the bank of river Gomati and tended by Krishna himself. Krishna in Vrindavan served me for the good of the world and the gopis, for the progress of Gokula, and for Kamsa's death.

The Puranas prescribe to the theory that I was planted on the order of Vashishta by Lord Rama. He planted me on the bank of the river Sarayu for killing the demons. I was pre-planted for progress in penance.

Devi Sita when abducted by Ravana meditated on me in Sri Lanka and was united with her Lord.

Goddess Parvati planted me in the Himalayas to increase her penance and to gain Lord Shankara as her consort. I am bound to serve others but blessed to be served by the wives of the Gods for the destruction of evil dreams.

Lord Rama planted me in the Dandaka forest and brother Lakshmana and Goddess Sita made sure to nourish me and protect me.

As river Ganga is glorified in the sacred texts, so is Tulsi in the Padma Purana.

Sugriva, while living in Rishyamukha, served me for destroying Vali, and Lord Hanuman offered his respect before crossing the sea and returning victorious in his mission.

Placing just on one leaf of Tulsi at the Lord's feet, transports you to Heaven and frees you from sins. He is freed from the murder of a brahmana. He, who bears on his head the water trickling down your lotus like leaf, obtains a bath in the Ganges, Oh Goddess.

～ VI.2 ～

Pativrata

I AM CHASTITY

Tulsi is the custodian of Vedas.
The rasa or juice of which is best: Surasa

यन् मुले सर्व तिर्तानि यनग्रे सर्वदेवता ।
यन् मध्येय् सर्व देवास्चे तुलसि त्वम् नमाम्यहम् ॥

I bow to the Tulsi at whose base are all the holy
places at whose middle are all deities
and on whose top reside all Vedas
We see Tulsi as the embodiment of everything

I lay enraptured, wholly consumed, beneath the night sky. My Lord Krishna has just made love to me for the first time and I feel cherished. There is no surprise more magical than the surprise of being loved…the only disadvantage being that it makes you hungry for more!

But alas, my bliss is short-lived! Lord Krishna's beloved Radha Rani spots me lying in a stupor in the aftermath of lovemaking and is furious. She curses me to take birth among the mortals.

A life on earth! I was disconsolate. Does it mean I will have to abandon Lord Krishna and his spiritual abode? How will I ever be able to endure this…but all is yet not lost. Lord Krishna arrives to pacify me, tells me not to lament and promises to unite with me on earth and marry me in his four-armed avatar as Narayana.

I often wonder if this would have occurred had I not experienced my Lord intimately, but then I would never have experienced an earthly incarnation, married Narayana, or cherished the meaning of abstinence in its purest sense.

I am Jatismara.

I have knowledge of my previous births. I remember that in my previous birth, I was a cowherd girl in Vrindavan and constant companion to supreme Goddess Radha, assisting her in the service of Lord Krishna.

I was reborn a special child on earth. My father, King Dharmadhvaja, ardently prayed to Goddess Lakshmi for her grace and Goddess Lakshmi fulfilled his desire. They say that when I was born, I resembled a celestial being. My feet had imprints of the lotus flower, my face was like the autumnal moon and a halo had settled around my body. I was Lakshmi incarnate.

As I grew to maturity I became devoted to Lord Krishna and for many years practiced extreme asceticism to attain him as a consort. In the blazing summer sun, I exposed myself to four fires; in the winter, I submerged myself in icy waters; and in the rainy season, I subjected myself to heavy downpours at the funeral grounds.

For 20,000 years, I subsisted on fruits and water; for 30,000 years, I chewed dry leaves; for 40,000 years I survived on air; and for 10,000 years I deprived myself of food, all the while performing tapasya standing erect on one leg.

I am commitment.

I am tradition.

I am truth.

Lord Krishna was my essence, my resolve, my perseverance, and I was going to have Him at any cost.

Finally, God Brahma appeared before me and asked me what I desired. I expressed my unquenchable yearning for Lord Krishna: I desired Krishna and all of him and none other than my Lord.

And Lord Brahma said, "Your time will come soon Tulsi and I assure you, you will be satiated." He elaborated that Radha had in the meanwhile cursed another resident of Vrindavan to take an earthly form. Sankhachuda, formerly Sudama, one of Lord Krishna's cowherd friends in Vrindavan, was presently living on earth among the demons.

"Sankhachuda has long wanted to marry you, so go to him for now and in time to come the Lord will accept you as his consort."

I was elated. Lord Krishna was my ultimate goal and I would leave no stone unturned to possess him.

I discovered that Sankhachuda, son of Dambha, was living as a powerful Danava who were hostile to the deities. When he entered his ascetic years, Sankhachuda remembered his attraction for me in his former life as Sudama. He learned that I too had taken birth as an earthly being.

Sankhachuda then appealed to Lord Brahma who granted him his wishes of being invincible to the Gods and to marry me. Lord Brahma blessed Sankhachuda with an amulet that once belonged to Lord Vishnu and was known to bestow success in all endeavours.

Sankhachuda's plight is so similar to mine! Surely there is a sign in that? Destiny is a strange journey.

I recall with clarity my first image of Sankhachuda. He was magnificent, God-like and astonishingly beautiful decorated with a garland of golden ornaments. I was stunned by his arresting appearance. Sankhachuda, too, beheld me and appeared at once smitten and proposed marriage to me.

Lord Brahma came to sanctify our union and blessed my husband on the condition that I remained chaste and faithful to him. I was surprised by his words for my loyalty has always been uncompromising. Chastity is innate to my nature.

For many thousands of years, we lived happily together. Sankhachuda grew unassailable by the power of Lord Vishnu's amulet and Lord Brahma's blessings, and our marital life was pure bliss. He began to rule the demons, the universe, and even the Gods. The deities were displeased. Sankhachuda had usurped their space. He dispossessed them of their realms and privileges, deprived them of their rights to worship and offerings; seized their weapons and ornaments. The Gods were frantic: something had to be done to rectify the situation.

Finally the frustrated Gods appealed to Lord Vishnu to seek his intervention in restoring the Heavenly universal order that had been taken over by the invincible Danava.

Lord Vishnu spoke reassuringly. "Sankhachuda was cursed by Radha Rani to become a Danava, but the curse is drawing to an end...It is time for him to return to the spiritual world." Lord Vishnu plotted Sankhachuda's fall while the Gods consolidated arms headed by Lord Shiva, assembled for battle and awaited for the Danava to emerge from his city.

Back inside our abode, Sankhachuda was preparing for a confrontation with the Gods. He was seething and I was beginning to feel uneasy. I said to him, "My Lord, I fear something ominous. I fear something terrible is about to unfold. Last night I had an inexplicable dream that filled me with anxiety. I saw you going to Death's abode and I have been frightened ever since. Stay with me for just a while and satisfy my eyes with your presence."

Sankhachuda gently stroked my head and said: "All of us must reap the results of our actions, good and bad. In time, trees grow, branches expand, and flowers blossom and fruits appear. But in time, the fruitful tree will also decay and the flowers will wilt. Similarly, human beings grow and decline. In time, the creator conceives, the preserver protects and the destroyer perishes. This is the law of creation, preservation and destruction. Nothing of this world will endure. Providence has brought us together and will again separate us. This cannot be avoided."

He was calm and unruffled.

I began to weep and held tightly onto my husband's hand. He continued speaking softly. "My beloved, it is not possible for me to be your everlasting shelter. I am but mortal. The only one who can offer you that is Krishna, the eternal Lord of all creatures. In him alone can you find peace and unending happiness".

He held me tightly against his chest while I sobbed. "We are both Lord Krishna's eternal slaves and we both know this. We come together because He desires and we part because He wills it. Accept the truth and submit to it. We need not mourn our parting for we shall soon return to him and our sorrows will be dissolved forever."

Sankhachuda rode out and told his charioteer to ride him to Lord Shiva. When he reached the all-powerful God, he descended from his vehicle and bowed reverentially. He also offered respect to Goddess Kali and to Shiva's son Kartikeya who was on his right.

A ferocious fight ensued between the two but Sankhachuda could not be slain by Kartikeya. Mata Kali rained her deadly weapons on him but Sankhachuda remained unblemished. As she began to invoke Pashupata, Shiva's most powerful weapon, a voice from the Heavens stopped her. "This Danava cannot be slain for as long as he wears the amulet and his wife remains chaste. Your weapon will do him no harm but destroy the world instead."

The prophecy held true. The battle continued for a full year relentlessly. My consort was a courageous warrior and I his faithful companion. He was a committed husband and I his chaste wife. My devotion to my husband empowered me with a force through which I was able to increase his strength and therefore, his lifespan. As long as I remain chaste, my husband will be invincible, indestructible.

One evening, when the fighting had ceased for the day, an old brahmana, really Lord Vishnu in disguise, approached my husband Sankhachuda. He asked the Danava for his amulet. Sankhachuda could never refuse the request of a brahmana and despite the implications he handed it over in charity. Destiny had cast the die and Sankhachuda understood that his end was near.

I didn't know this then but Lord Vishnu disappeared from the battlefield temporarily and assumed Sankhachuda's appearance. He arrived at our abode unannounced and I was overjoyed to see—who I thought was my husband—after so many months.

"My Lord, you are back from the war. Finally our

troubles are over but how did you manage to defeat the deities headed as they were by Lord Shiva? I have been so worried for you, prayed for you incessantly but thank our stars that you are back hale and hearty. I am proud to be your consort, proud of your valour and victory."

Lord Vishnu shared details of the battle to not raise suspicion of his identity and lovingly led me to our bed chamber. We lay down on the bejewelled bed and after a long separation made passionate love.

The curse had come true: I had been unfaithful to my consort. Now there was nothing to protect Sankhachuda from the wrath of the deities on the battlefront. He had finally been rendered I am vulnerable.

I am passion.

I am poetry.

I am worship.

Lord Vishnu was back on the battleground and Lord Shiva estimated it was time to crush Sankhachuda with his trident. This divine weapon was capable of destroying an entire universe. It glowed like the sun as Shiva hurled it straight at the Danava.

Sankhachuda acknowledge his end as Lord Shiva's trident flew towards him. He knew that the trident could not be thwarted and sat down upon the battlefield in a yogic posture, meditating on Lord Krishna and preparing for his end. The trident circled him three times before impaling him to death.

A cry of victory went up from the Gods. Their deadliest

enemy was slain. Lord Shiva then took up Sankhachuda's bones and threw them into the ocean. "These bones shall become the sacred conch shells used in prayer everywhere." It is believed that wherever and whenever the conch is blown, Goddess Lakshmi makes it a point to dwell inside the shell. The water inside the conch is regarded as sacred as the holy river and can be offered to all the demigods except to Lord Shiva because he is the vanquisher.

Lord Shiva may have finally demolished Sankhachuda but he was proud of his valour, appreciative of his earnestness. And it is for these reasons that Shiva released Sankhachuda of his curse. Sankhachuda the Danava transformed into his original self Sudama, the cowherd. Mounted on a divine chariot adorned with jewels and holding a flute, surrounded by his cowherd friends, Sankhachuda weightlessly flew into the spiritual sky as his soul rose up toward the supreme transcendental abode.

There, Radha and Lord Krishna welcomed him and revived their eternal pastimes together.

I cannot see them anymore but I sense them in my day-to-day existence. Sankhachuda was right. We have to move with time. As my consort, he prepared me for my metamorphosis. There was the pain of losing him but there was happiness of reuniting with my Lord. Lord Krishna is right: everything moves according to destiny and we have no choice but to accept our Karma.

Vishnupriya

I AM BELOVED

Tulsi is dear to Lord Vishnu.
One that bears many clusters of flowers or
inflorescences: Bahumanjari

नमस्तुलसी कल्याणी नमो विष्णुप्रिये ।
शुभे नमो मोक्षप्रदे देवी नमः सम्पत्प्रदायिनी ॥

I bow to auspicious Tulsi who is dear to Lord Vishnu
Who brings good luck to devotees
Who guides one to attain salvation
Who showers all the wealth to the devotees

The man lying beside me on my bed in the chamber was not my husband. His embraces were not the same.

"Who are you?" I asked fearfully looking in his direction. "You are surely not my husband. Whoever you are, you have deceived me...taken advantage of me."

Lord Vishnu instantly assumed his own true beautiful form, with four arms and a complexion resembling the blue lotus. Here was the Lord of the demigods standing before me! Dressed in his characteristic yellow robe and many divine ornaments, he was dazzling.

But I was devastated. If Lord Vishnu himself could be so devious, what hope was left for the world! "O Lord, why did you deceive me and violate my purity as a ploy to kill my husband…Is this fair and does it suit you to be so manipulative? I have worshipped you all my life. How could you do this to your staunch devotee? Your devotee committed no offence and yet, for the sake of others, you killed him! I have committed no wrong and yet you killed my consort! Why? You have shown the heartlessness of a stone. I therefore curse you to become one."

Lord Vishnu was conciliatory. "Exalted one, do you not recall how you performed austerities for a lifetime to obtain me as your husband? Well Sankhachuda also performed austerities for a lifetime to obtain you as his wife. By that austerity, I fulfilled his wish. It was then necessary for me to fulfil yours. For this reason, I did what I did."

As I continued to sob, Lord Vishnu gently explained. "It is time for you, Tulsi, to leave your earthly body and regain your spirituality. It is time for you to be married to me…To stand by my side as my consort Lakshmi. Your body will transform into a famous river Gandaki, virtuous, pure, and transparent. Your lustrous hair will take the shape of holy Tulsi trees. The residents of the three worlds will henceforth worship your plant; revere the leaves and the flowers. From now on, you, Tulsi, will reign as the best among trees and flowers."

I was ecstatic, but dismayed all the while.

Lord Vishnu empathised with my conflict. He acknowledged my curse to become a stone. "I will transform into a stone and remain close to the bank of the river Gandaki. Millions of Vajrakita worms, with their sharp teeth, will make convolutions or rings in the stones there, representing me. These will be known as Shaligrama or sacred stones and will be used for worship. Indeed this will always be done with Tulsi leaves. So never again shall we be parted, either in this world or my spiritual abode."

Lord Vishnu said that wherever there are Shaligrama stones, Lord Hari will exist too. And wherever Lord Hari is, Goddess Lakshmi and all the holy places also exist.

"He who worships the Shaligrama without Tulsi leaves, or he who dares to separate the leaves from the stone, will have to suffer separation from his wife in his next birth. He who does not offer the Tulsi leaves inside a conch, remains without a partner for seven births and becomes diseased. He, who maintains the Shaligrama sila, the Tulsi, and the conch in one place, becomes very dear to Lord Narayana."

Thus, I was finally restored to my original spiritual consciousness, my true calling, and my justification.

I cast off my anger and abandoned my body and followed my Lord to his eternal domain.

And so it goes. Tradition paints my love affair with Lord Vishnu as an intense one tied to the Gandaki river of Nepal, where we made love. Shaligrama stones found in the bed of river Gandaki are considered the sperm of Lord Vishnu and they are a critical element in his worship.

Since then I am considered the central sectarian symbol of the Vaishnavites; the manifestation of the God in the vegetable kingdom.

It is with my wood that a light is burned for Lord Vishnu, which is the equivalent of burning several hundred thousand other lights in his honour. It is with my leaves that a paste is prepared and applied on a devotee's body before praying to Lord Vishnu and this one day exercise is equivalent of a hundred ordinary worships. Without my leaves no ceremony in honour of Lord Vishnu is ever complete. Food offered to the Lord without Tulsi is unacceptable to Lord Vishnu.

Vaishnavites traditionally use Japa Malas made from Tulsi stems or roots, which are an important symbol of initiation. Tulsi beads are considered to be auspicious for the wearer, and believed to put them under the protection of Lords Vishnu and Krishna. They have such a strong association with Vaishnavites, that followers of Lord Vishnu have long been called "those who bear the Tulsi round the neck."

The Vaishnavites also worship the Lord's incarnations, Rama and Krishna. Sometimes a devotee fasts while offering 100,000 Tulsi leaves to Lord Krishna, placing them one by one at the Lord's feet. Sometimes, pilgrims visit holy places like Dwarka, Lord Krishna's capital in Gujarat, carrying me in their palms for the entire pilgrimage.

I am sacred to Lord Shiva as well. During Parthiva Puja time of Shiva worship, the black earth that goes to make his linga is taken from beneath my plant.

But it doesn't end there!

Our union is so precious that it has been solemnised in marriage. I am ceremonially married to Lord Vishnu annually on the eleventh bright day of the month of Kartika in the Hindu calendar. The Chaturmasya begins right after the bright fortnight of the eleventh day of Sadh or Sayani Ekadasi or "sleeping eleventh" when Lord Vishnu retires to sleep in a vast ocean on the back of his serpent Ananta. The next four months are considered inauspicious and come to an end on Prabhodani Ekadasi or "waking eleventh."

On this day, my vivaah with Lord Vishnu is performed by planting both of us in the same pot. This heralds an end to the inauspicious period popularly known as shraddha and also opens up the marriage season and auspicious life-cycle in the Hindu calendar.

Like Lord Vishnu, Lord Krishna too figures prominently in the month of Kartik. Several followers attribute the sum total of his life as a cowherd in Braj, from his birth to his eventual departure and this culminates in the Krishnalila performed on the Tulsi Ghat on the twelfth of Kartik's darkest fortnight and ending just at month's end.

Every evening during Kartika, people light lamps and worship me, for I am auspicious for their homes.

I am Haripriya.

I am Vishnupriya.

I am dear to Lord Vishnu.

Where there is Tulsi there is Vishnu, too.

Blessings of the Shaligrama

And Lord Hari continued…

By worshiping the Shaligrama sila, one destroys the sin of having killed a brahmana and any other type of sin.

If one observes vows, offers gifts, consecrates a temple, performs sraddha or funeral ceremonies, or pays obeisance to the demigods before the Shaligrama sila–all these acts become highly exalted.

If one prays to the Shaligrama sila, one acquires the merits of bathing in all the tirthas and being initiated into all the Vedic sacrifices.

Furthermore, one acquires all the merits acquired by performing all the Vedic sacrifices by visiting all the holy places, by fulfilling vows, by practicing all austerities and by reading all the Vedas.

Whoever performs his abhisheka ceremony always with Shaligrama water—being sprinkled with this water at the initiation and installation ceremonies—acquires the spiritual merits gained by offering all sorts of gifts and walking around the entire earth.

Without a doubt, the demigods are pleased with the person who worships the Shaligrama sila daily. He becomes so holy that even all the holy places desire his touch. He becomes a Jivanmukta and very godly. Ultimately he goes to Vaikuntha and serves Lord Hari there eternally. Any sin, such as the killing of a brahmana, flies away from him just as snakes flee at the sight of garuda. The earth is consecrated by the dust of his feet. By his birth, he redeems one hundred thousand of his ancestors.

Anyone who, while dying, drinks the Shaligrama sila water, will be freed from all his sins and go to Vaikuntha. He becomes completely freed from the effects of karma and becomes absorbed in the vision of Lord Vishnu's feet.

~ VI.4 ~

Lakshmi

I AM PROSPERITY
One that flourishes in open land, especially
in the villages: Gramya

आदित्यवर्णे तपसोऽधिजातो वनस्पतिस्तव वृक्षोऽथ बिल्वः ।
तस्य फलानि तपसानुदन्तु मायान्तरायाश्च बाह्या अलक्ष्मीः ॥

Sri Suktam

O Universal Mother, shining like sun
It is through your penance that the holiest trees
of Bilva and Tulsi are born
They symbolise the tree of life
The fruit of that tree of life removes our poverty
from both within and without
In other words, bless us with inner light and
outer independence and abundance

131

It is the full moon night of sarat poornima that launches Kartik celebrations. It is the night when Goddess Lakshmi, quintessential Goddess of auspiciousness, is invoked with extreme fervour. Innumerable sky lamps are placed in tiny baskets and hoisted on the top of bamboo poles, forming a beautiful sight on the ghats along the banks of the Ganges. It is believed that Goddess Lakshmi herself will come to view these lamps and bestow health, wealth, and prosperity on her devotees.

I am fortunate that every time a lamp is lit to welcome Goddess Lakshmi, I am included in the prayers as well.

There is an interesting story about my past. When I left my physical body and assumed a celestial form, I was transported to Vaikuntha. There, I resided in the heart of Lord Vishnu, close to Goddess Lakshmi, one of the Lord's wives. The Lord duly honoured me, elevating me to the rank of his spouse and I felt very nurtured and blessed.

Goddess Saraswati however was not pleased with the importance Lord Vishnu accorded me and made her displeasure apparent. Offended by her behaviour, I disappeared from the Heavenly abode. Lord Vishnu, not finding me in Heaven went desperately searching for me everywhere till he was exhausted and stopped in a forest to rest for a while.

At a little distance he spotted a pond and decided to bathe and offer his prayers. Next, he meditated on me with extreme devotion. So intense were his prayers, that I could no more curb my longing for him and lured out of the

132

bushes, fell at my Lord's feet. He clasped me to his breast and carried me with him to Goddess Saraswati. He reconciled our differences and in the presence of all he declared that henceforth he will carry me with him forever, on his head and at his feet there will be Tulsi forever.

And he kept his promise.

Goddess Saraswati, humbled by the Lord's feelings for me, embraced me and made a place for me beside her, Goddesses Lakshmi and Ganga finally took me home with them.

I am Lakshmipriya, dear to Lakshmi. She resides next to the Shaligrama, by the side of Lord Vishnu and therefore I am never far away from my beloved.

But sometimes, I am Goddess Lakshmi, wife of Lord Vishnu, so anyone who worships me with sincerity will reap my benediction.

I am wealth, I am prosperity, and I am light.

The courtyard of a traditional home is my sacred space and most Hindu families build a special structure - an eight-petalled lotus or Ashtadhalam to plant me. It is a unique nesting spot with a small space to light an oil lamp and the lamp is usually lit by the lady of the house every day at twilight.

During my vivaah to Lord Vishnu I become an incarnation of Goddess Lakshmi and I spread my aura of munificent benevolence to the house, bringing plenty and prosperity.

The vivaah is an elaborate five-day festival and the rituals are performed in the evening. My devotees observe fasts for the entire day and at dusk dress me up as a bride. They bring branches of amla and sugarcane and tie them to me, attach all the symbols of marital bliss: the chunri, bangle, mangalsutra, sindoor, and flowers. The pundit chants the Vedic mantras and at the auspicious muhurat, the sacred marriage is performed.

Several dishes are prepared in my honour and prasad is distributed among the guests and the devotees.

Thus I become Goddess Lakshmi, wife of Vishnu. My marriage symbolises a realisation of my identity; it is the completion of my destiny and most important, it marks the auspicious beginning of the marriage season for Hindus.

There are innumerable stories of my past and all very intriguing…

Once, Goddess Saraswati and Goddess Lakshmi quarrelled bitterly. They cursed one another and Saraswati's curse transformed Lakshmi into a Tulsi plant that forced her to live on earth forever. Lord Vishnu was anguished. He intervened and said that Lakshmi will live her curse in the world but as a Holy Tulsi and when the period of the curse is completed, she will return to his abode as his consort.

I am wealth, I am prosperity, I am light.

And till this time, he will wait for her by the riverside in the form of Shaligrama sila. The sila deities and the Tulsi plant are thus always worshipped together as Vishnu and Lakshmi.

So I am fortune, fertility, I am generosity.

On the twelfth day of the brighter half of the month of Kartik, all Vaishnavites have a ritual of performing the marriage of Tulsi to the Shaligrama.

I am the embodiment of beauty; I am grace and charm.

In one of her previous births, Goddess Rukmini, wife of Lord Krishna, was born as Gunawati who worshipped me with extreme devotion. So great was her piety that her house became endowed with the presence of all eight forms of Lakshmi.

Rukmini o Rukmini! I will bless you for your attachment! Not all the wealth and ornaments of Satyabhama will outweigh Lord on the tulabharam! But if you place a single leaf of mine on the pan I assure you it will tilt the scale.

~ VI.5 ~

Parampara

I AM RITUAL

Tulsi extinguishes sin.
At its very sight, demonic diseases or sins
vanish away—Apat Rakshati

ओम् छम्पे यनसि कयै नमः
ओम् कनबु सुन्दर गलयै नमः
ओम् ततिल्ल तंग्यै नमः

ओम् मत्त भन्दराकुन्ता लयै नम:
ओम् नक्षत्र निभानि खयै नम:
ओम् रम्भानि भोरु युग्मायै नम:
ओम् साईकट श्रोन्यै नम:
ओम् मधकान्ति रव मद्ययै नम:
ओम् कीरवन्यै नम:
ओम् श्रीमहा तुल्स्यै नम:

Samkshipt Padma Purana

**Worshipping, reciting, meditating, planting
and wearing of Tulsi
Bestows Heaven and liberation
He who imparts and practices Tulsi worship
Finds the supreme place, the abode of Madhava**

Oh, Holy Tulsi,
Bosom friend of Lakshmi
Destroyer of sins
Bestower of blessings
Salutations to thee
who is praised by sage Narada
and is the darling of Lord Narayana
I am Vrinda.
I am worship.

Every morning the lady of the house begins her day with
me.

Her chanting is ceaseless, her focus unwavering as she

walks around me, worshipping me with passion, watering me intermittently. Every day I am dressed in a fragrant garland of flowers and kumkum is applied on my leaves. On special days, she adorns me with a piece of red cloth and offers me a red flower; then she resumes her circumambulation and sings me a special aarti.

Over the centuries we have formed a bond. She has understood that all I need is a little sunlight, a little water and a heart soaked in sincerity. I gorge on her devotion. I am the first to be greeted after her daily bath and the last to be bowed to at dusk. Her communion with me is perpetual. Day upon day, year after year, she lights a lamp for me and murmurs a silent prayer. She says she feels incomplete when she doesn't because just being around me cleanses her mind of all the dross.

I am as accustomed to her as she to me. I relish her reverence and though neither of us communicate we feel connected in a strange, silent way. I can always sense when she is anguished in the way she stands before me and folds her hands. I can sense what's worrying her and I try and absolve her suffering as quickly as I can.

She relies on me for my tradition. I rely on her for her devotion.

In a quiet, unspoken way we are sensitised to each other. She understands my fragility and nurtures me so I don't wither away. Sometimes, as she circulates I wonder what makes her so devoted. Does she perceive me as Goddess Lakshmi or as Lord Vishnu incarnate? Does she think I am the spirit of the universe or does she think I am just a century old tradition to be passed on to successive generations?

I will never know because we never talk, in our silence however we share a bond where I am sometimes her conscience and sometimes her alter ego. In all probabilities I am just tradition for her, a virtue she has inculcated out of habit.

I am probably her reflection or probably her salvation. I am her mother, her custodian and a good luck charm... the continuity of a custom. She relates to me in every role in every which way.

Her penance culminates in the ultimate act of obeisance: she plucks a leaf as she chants devoutly and chews me up.

She has subsumed my spirit into her being. She has become me.

She receives me with all my paradoxes. I am purity but I am also a lover. I am the Goddess but I am also the earth. I am ritual and I am also contemporary. I am devotion; I am love, responsibility, steadfast loyalty. I symbolise the virtues and miseries of my gender. I am Hindu femininity. I am the Indian woman.

So, here I am a lasting symbol of Hindu culture.

The courtyards of Hindu households are my domain and it is my responsibility to spread my spirituality and promote the material prosperity and wellbeing of the household.

Hindus have revered me from time immemorial and have faith in my auspicious presence. During the four months of the monsoon period called Chaturmas, they worship me with a ritual and transform me from a mere plant to the divine representative of Lord Vishnu or Lord Krishna. It is believed that any home I grace transforms in to a place of pilgrimage where no disease or messengers of Yama can trespass.

I am one of the few surviving symbols of Indian tradition. I evoke a spontaneous reverence. I am inconspicuous in my presence and undemanding in my rituals. I don't discriminate among my devotees and don't choose my place of worship. I am there for whoever cherishes me and as along as they can nurture me.

My devotees understand this and find it easier to adopt me than perform demanding rituals. I am privileged to have the ancient religious texts praise me to the skies!

My benefits are plentiful and profuse. People who breathe my fragrance benefit spiritually. Those who plant me and care for me are absolved of their sins. Even by growing just one of me, the presence of Lords Vishnu, Brahma, Mahesh and other Gods is assured. Praying to me is like accruing the benefits of a pilgrimage. If I am grown during Kartik month, the accumulated sins of many births are absolved. Salvation is the prize for offering me to the Lord.

Whoever consumes me thrice daily achieves purity. Bathing in my water is akin to bathing at pilgrim centres. When a person is dying, he is fed my leaves dipped in Ganga water. I am partial to Kartik; donating my leaves during this month is equivalent to Godaan or the gift of a cow to a brahmana.

Whosoever wears my beads gets the fruit of Aswamedh Yagna. Tulsi mritika or the earth beneath me is sacred and if anybody besmears his body with it attains the merits of a yogi.

The Vishnustuti Nairs of Kerala make seven circumambulations of Vrindavan or Tulsi thara after bathing. And the Vaishnavites of Uttar Pradesh conduct their entire pilgrimage nursing me in the palms of their hands.

Everybody knows that Vishnu, the Lord of the three worlds, takes up abode in the village or the house where I am cultivated. The house in which I reside is free from calamities like poverty, illness, or separation from dear ones. I am the holiest plant and without my leaves, Lord Vishnu will not accept any ceremonial worship or offering. I am the destroyer of all evils and it is sinful to break my branches.

I am Vaishnavite. The Bhaktamala states that, "Those who wear Tulsi around their necks, the rosary of Lotus seeds, carry the conch shell and discus impressed upon their upper arms, and the upright white and pink streaks on their foreheads, are Vaishnavas, and they sanctify the world."

I am worshipped for different reasons. A widow worships me for salvation. The young girl prays to me for a good husband. Couples pray for children and the elderly worship me to attain Heaven after death.

By hearing or recalling the Tulsi hymn, a son will be born to the sonless woman, a wife will be obtained by the wifeless man, health will be restored to a diseased person, freedom will be given to a prisoner, fearlessness will be bestowed upon the terrified, and salvation will be granted to the sinners.

Whoever worships me with my eight names acquires the merit of performing an Ashvamedha sacrifice.

I collect in many groups, and therefore I am called Vrinda.

I was noticed in the Vrindavan forest and came to be recognised as Vrindavani.

I am worshipped throughout the world and recognised as Visvapujita.

I purify the whole universe, so I am Visvapavani.

I am the essence of all flowers, therefore I am called Puspasara.

My attainment brings faith and joy making me Nandini.

I am incomparable, I am Tulsi.

I am the life of Sri Krishna and therefore Krishnajivani.

Lord Narayana has a better way to surmise me.

"You will always be the presiding deity of the Tulsi plant on Earth, and at the same time you will accompany Sri Krishna in solitude in Goloka…You will be the presiding deity of the river Gandaki, and shower India with religious merit… You will be the wife of the ocean of salt, which is my partial expansion… O chaste Goddess, you will always remain personally by my side and enjoy my company, as Lakshmi does…"

~ VI.6 ~

Vishwaas

I AM BELIEF

Tulsi is symbol of regeneration.

One that destroys demons: Bhutagni

तुलसि दल मात्रेना
जलस्य कुलुकेन व ।
विक्रिनिते स्वम् आत्मनम
भक्तेब्यह्यो भक्तवत्सला ॥

Gautamya Tantra, the Hari Bhakti Vilasa

The Lord who is fond of His devotees
Submits himself for a mere leaf of Tulsi or
A drop of water held in the palm
With sharp taste and bitter aftertaste,
Hot, light, and dry in effect,
It cures ailments originating in kapha and vayu,
It stimulates hunger and improves digestion,
It sharpens the intellect and grants
spiritual ennoblement,
It improves vision and benefits the heart,
It imparts flavour and disseminates fragrance.

A man taking basil from a woman will love her always.

–Sir Thomas More

I am Vrindavani.

I am Viswapawni.

It is said that everyone in this universe has a soul mate but only the fortunate few discover them. Perhaps I am among those few. Let me elaborate it with a mesmerising tale from medieval Italy, the love story of Lisabetta and Lorenzo.

Lisabetta belonged to a noble family while Lorenzo was a poor man, an employee of Lisabetta's brothers. When they discovered that their sister was in love with their employee, they were outraged and proceeded to murder him.

In the meantime Lisabetta was distraught at Lorenzo's sudden disappearance but her brothers did not reveal their dark secret to her. Sorrowful and frightened, she asked no questions but silently cried for him. Many a night she called out piteously to him, pleading into the darkness that he return to her.

Until one day, Lorenzo appeared to Lisabetta in a dream. He informed Lisabetta of his fate and how he was manipulated and killed by her brothers. When Lisabetta finally learned that the love of her life has been killed, she plunged into grief. She yearned to see Lorenzo again, unwilling to accept that this was the end.

She ventured out in search of Lorenzo and finally discovered his battered body buried in the ground. Lisabetta was distraught by the cruelty and broke down. Finding the sorrow of parting too painful, she pulled out Lorenzo's head from his body and carried him home.

In the privacy of her room, Lisabetta placed her beloved's head inside a pot where she could look at him from all corners of the room. Lisabetta now wrapped the new plant in a piece of fine cloth, and set it inside a large and beautiful vessel. She then covered it with earth and in it she grew a Tulsi plant. Lisabetta sat before the plant and wept all day drenching the plant with her tears. Fostered with such constant, unremitting care, the Tulsi grew vigorously, nourished by Lisabetta's tears but she gradually withered away.

Over time, the burgeoning Tulsi became the embodiment of Lorenzo.

Lisabetta's family was concerned about her reclusive behaviour. They were baffled by her attachment to a plant and unaware of the mystery, stole the pot in an effort to remedy her despair. It was a fatal mistake! For Lisabetta, the Tulsi plant had become Lorenzo. And when it was taken from her, she died of sorrow.

There is a feeling of déjà vu to this tale from medieval Italy. It has echoes of my passion and tragedy. Perhaps it is my destiny that I intersect cultures and beliefs. It is my destiny that I traverse civilizations and traditions. My story has been prortrayed in books and in films in India and abroad.

Let there be no doubt about my true calling: I am the

paramour of Lord Vishnu. Would I have this privilege if Goddess Lakshmi had not cursed me into becoming a plant and the Lord not transformed himself into the sacred Shaligrama sila to keep me company? This gesture remains for me His ultimate expression of love!

I am embedded in passion. I was born out of it and my story is shaped by it, too. I am the symbol of new life and regeneration.

I am an inherent part of Hindu rituals and prayer and water mixed with my leaves is equivalent to the holy Ganges, but what is intriguing is that I have significance in Christianity as well. The Bible narrates that I was found growing around Lord Jesus' tomb after His resurrection. It says that when women came to plant Myrrh and spices on the tomb of the fallen Saviour for preservation, they did not find a corpse but an empty tomb and some fresh Tulsi leaves. In the Greek Orthodox Church I am assigned a central role in the festive celebration of the birth of St. Basil and mingled in the preparation of the holy water to be offered to the Lord.

In India, I am placed in the mouth of the deceased to ensure they attain salvation. In Europe, they place me in the hands of the dead to ensure a safe journey to Heaven. The ancient Egyptians and the Greeks believe that I have the powers to open the gates of Heaven.

I am ritual...I am renewal.

I am Tulsi-mata, presiding in the courtyards of Hindu households as I spread my spirituality and promote the material prosperity of the household.

Jewish folklore suggests I add strength while fasting. I am a symbol of love in Italy and a symbol of mourning in ancient Greece. The European lore claims that I am a symbol of Satan and the African legend believes that I protect against scorpions, while others aver that smelling too much of me would breed scorpions in the brain!

I am belief... I am conviction.

I am an aphrodisiac to some and am associated with pagan love used in love spells. In Italy, a variety of sweet basil named "Kiss Me Nicholas," is associated with spouse attraction. Sometimes, a pot of me on a windowsill is meant to signal a lover. In ancient European folklore, there is a superstition that when a man accepts a sprig of basil from a woman, he will fall in love with her.

In fact the basil is a determining factor in marriage ceremonies. The old guards believe that before determining a liaison you place two fresh basil leaves upon a live coal. If they burn quickly to ashes, the marriage will be harmonious but if they crackle, the couple is bound to face turbulence and if the leaves fly apart with fierce crackling, it means the relationship is undesirable.(Cunningham)

I am compassion.

I am love.

In India, I grant husbands and children. One, who places my leaves on his chest at bed time, will be freed of the evil spirits from dreams. For the Jews, I am carried as a spray for their chests when they attend religious feasts in Israel. The folklore says that one, who carries my leaves, attract wealth.

I have been associated with the planet Mars and the element of Fire.

I am purity.

I am fertility.

I am a good luck charm.

I am Basileus, I am royalty.

~๑ VI.7 ๑~

Jiva-Agni

I AM LIFE-GIVER

Tulsi heals and uplifts.

One endowed with a large variety of different kinds of virtues: Barbari.

तुलस्यमृत जन्मसि सदा त्वम् केसवप्रिया ।
केसवर्ति सिनोमि त्वम् बरदा भव शोबिने ॥

O Tulsi, you were born from nectar
You are always very dear to Lord Keshava
Now, in order to worship Lord Keshava, I am
collecting your leaves and manjaris
Please bestow your benediction on me

The wind that carries my fragrance spreads health and wellbeing wherever it blows.

Among humans, it is the saatviks the knowledge-givers and protectors, the kind and generous who earn the highest respect and love. Humans transcend instinct into the realm of intelligence to discover truth beyond bodily concerns.

I am saatvik.

I am evolved.

I am consciousness.

I impart goodness and healing both physically and spiritually. I aid growth, evolvement.

I am divinity.

My instinct works beyond the mind and stimulates the soul. I radiate energy that protects and heals. I am the gateway to life. I absorb the cosmic forces in the form of light and transform them into life. We transform light into life through photosynthesis; humans transform life into consciousness through perception.

The similarities are not coincidental! The human soul evolves from us plants. Humans are dependent on plants for survival and so have a profound connection to us.

A healthy relationship with nature transmits into a healthy society.

I am disappointed that humans no longer live in harmony with nature, this is the reason we experience an ecological imbalance today. Every time there is decay and deterioration in the environment, it is a signal that humans are losing contact with the laws of nature.

The growing industries and factories bring a new set of problems. Today life has become diseased and soil fertility is destroyed. Deforestation and global warming have led to drought and pollution. The problems are endless. The solution lies in nature, in us plants.

While many homes and workplaces preserve me, few are aware of my ecological significance. It is a tragedy that humans have lost their equilibrium with nature! Had they been aware, this could have been prevented.

Man derives oxygen from plants, he derives carbohydrates, proteins; minerals, vitamins, and even the water in the human body is traced back to plants. We are all extensions of the cosmic force of life. I help humans to reconnect with nature and with the cosmic intelligence to find the balance and harmony again.

Sometimes, I wonder what makes me so profound. Is it that extra electrical energy in my genes?

A dead body will not decay rapidly if placed among a cluster of my plants. This perhaps explains the religious ritual of putting my leaves in the mouth of a deceased. My energy purifies the air and invokes good spirits. I am the classic giving tree. Every part of me—my root, leaves, seeds, and bark—is used during cremation.

I radiate exuberance. If you wear my rosaries, you will attain peace as it helps in the elimination of the baser instincts. The charanamrit distributed in temples is soaked in my leaves and helps to pacify excited and choleric minds. The wind that has touched a Tulsi plant nurtures sacred thoughts and godliness.

I am trained to absorb positive ions, skilful at energising negative ions, and help to protect the ozone layer. It is believed that the oxygen I exhale contains over-powered molecules of three atoms instead of the regular atmospheric oxygen which has only two atoms.

It is my ability to foster a mind-body connection that makes me special. When I am used in the cure of an illness, it is the ritual associated with my use that becomes a spiritual component of my efficacy.

I affect the energy in humans; I balance their chakras. I connect with the "third eye." I open up the heart and the mind and bestow love and devotion. I strengthen faith, compassion and clarity. I give the protection of the divine by clearing the aura and strengthening the immune system.

As Lord Shiva observed, "Oh Narada, wherever Tulsi grows, there will be no misery for she is the holiest of the holy. The breeze surrounding her will always be pure and fragrant. I feel privileged because Vishnu showers me with his blessings. I am sacred because Brahma resides in the roots, Vishnu in my stems and leaves and Rudra in the flowering tops…"

The seers have confirmed that I contain natural mercury, which is the semen of Lord Shiva. It has the power of pure awareness, increases prana and sensory acuity. It removes kapha from the lungs and vata from the colon; my tea leaves mixed with honey brings satiation.

During the Satya Narayana puja a thousand leaves of mine are processed by the device of mantra alone and then

150

offered to Lord Vishnu. A sweet dish called sheera cooked of wheat berries in ghee and sprinkled with my leaves is offered to ignite the agni and a deep process of life-extending rejuvenation ensues.

Open up to my energies! I embody the forces of nature.

~ VI.8 ~

Rasayana

I AM HEALER
Tulsi is traditional and scientific
One that alleviates pain: Shoolaghni

महाप्रसाद जननी सर्वसौभाग्यवर्धिनी ।
आधि व्याधि जरा मुक्तं तुलसी त्वाम् नमोस्तुते ॥

O Mother Tulsi who bestows the fruit of devotion
Who brings good luck
Who alleviates sadness and heals disease
O Mother Tulsi I prostrate before you

"Health is a state of complete physical, mental, and social wellbeing and not merely absence of disease or infirmity." (World Health Organization)

I am the product of thousands of years of empirical evidence and use. I arouse the body; the senses and the nervous system. By consuming me spiritually and physically, human beings strive for a balance and harmony and open themselves up to the cosmic energy of the universe.

I am Rasayana.

A herb that nourishes perfect health and promotes long life. For perhaps 5000 years or more I hold legendary status among India's healing herbs. From general well-being to acute critical imbalance, I have a remedy for all.

I am Sattva.

I have the energy of purity – capable of eliciting goodness, virtue and joy in humans. Everything associated with me is holy, including water fed to me, the soil in which I grow my leaves, flowers, seed, and roots. I embody interconnectedness between all living things.

I am ancient.

I am contemporary.

I have a long history of medicinal use. I am mentioned in the oldest ancient Sanskrit Ayurvedic text, Charak Samhita, written perhaps in 600 BC, and even in the Rig-Veda, thought to have been written around 5000 BC.

I am Kalyani.

I am difficult to ignore!

While most herbs have limited use, I am recommended for hundreds of serious disorders. The ancient rishis recognised my proclivity for health and healing and declared me God! I became, in the process, one of the eight indispensable items for any Vedic worship ritual.

Today I am classified as a primary adaptogenic herb, a natural plant remedy that rejuvenates the body and increases vital energy. I improve the body's ability to resist stress, thereby improving health and preventing and treating disease. I contain alkaloids and glycosides. My leaves contain ascorbic acid and carotene. These compounds possess strong anti-oxidant, anti-bacterial, anti-viral, and immunity-enhancing properties that promote immunity against germs, stress and disease.

I am traditional.

I am also scientific.

I heal spiritually but modern chemistry has corroborated my powers to destroy microorganisms. I am useful in treating coughs, colds, fevers, headaches, lung problems, abdominal distention, absorption, arthritis, gas, memory loss, nasal ailment, nerve tissue strengthening, sinus, congestion, in clearing the lungs, and as a heart tonic. I also hold the capacity to strengthen the kidneys, the heart, and diminish cholesterol levels. What other herb can claim to have benefits for hundreds of conditions with thousands of years of empirical experience and use?

I am anti-bacterial.

I am insecticidal.

It is the oil in my leaves that gives me my fragrance. During an eclipse there is a tradition of placing my leaves in food and drink that have to be stored because my energy prevents their decay.

I free the ozone from the sun's rays which helps to oxygenate the body and cleanses the brain and the nerves. I relieve depression, the effects of poisons and difficult urination. I prevent the accumulation of fat in the body, obstinate skin diseases, arthritis, rheumatism, and initial stages of many types of cancer.

I contain traces of mineral and copper needed to absorb iron. My leaves are included in most of the herbal nerve-tonics. I am a repellent of flies, mosquitoes and insects, and valuable in combating malarial fever.

I am holistic.

I am stress-resilient.

Modern scientific research proposes that I have many benefits and that consuming me slows the biological aging process and reduces the cell and tissue damage caused by harmful rays of the sun, television, computers, X-rays, radiation therapy, high altitude air travel and more.

I am light.

I am antibiotic.

I offer antiviral and antifungal protection and I am useful in localised infections as well. I decrease the likelihood of strokes.

I am medical.

I am nutritious.

I contain vitamins C and A, minerals calcium, zinc, and iron, and chlorophyll and many other phytonutrients. I am also an allopathic medicine complement. I resolve dental and periodontal health, diminish bad breath, and speed healing of bone fractures, reduce nausea and cramping, and repel insects, including mosquitoes and lice.

As my devotees concur, "Of all flowers, Tulsi is the best. She is divine and beautiful, and burns up the fuel of sins like a flame of fire. Of all the goddesses, she is the most sacred. Because she is incomparable, she is called Tulsi. I worship this Goddess who is entreated by all. She is placed on the heads of all, desired by all, and makes the universe holy. She bestows liberation from this world and devotion to Lord Hari. I worship her."

I promote longevity and for this reason sometimes I am called the "elixir of life."

मौलौ मायूरबर्हं मृगमदतिलकं चारु लालाटपट्टे
कर्णद्वन्द्वे च तालीदलमतिमृदुलं मौक्तिकं नासिकायाम् ।
हारो मन्दारमालापरिमलभरिते कौस्तुभस्योपकण्ठे
पाणौ वेणुश्च यस्य व्रजयुवतियुतः पातु पीताम्बरो नः ॥

May that Krishna, who wears bright yellow pitambar,
who gives company to the belles of Vraja
Who adorns his head with the plumes of the peacock
and sports a tilak of deer musk on his pretty forehead
Who wears ear-ornaments of soft palm leaves, who has
nose-studs of pearls, who wears garlands of fragrant
mandara flowers and Kaustubha around the neck
Who carries a flute in his hand, protect us!

मुरारिणा वारिविहारकाले
मृगेक्षणानां मुषितांशुकानाम् ।
करद्वयम् वा कचसंहतिर्वा
प्रमीलनं वा परिधानमासीत् ॥

When, during water sports with the doe-eyed damsels of
Vraja, Murari stole their clothes, the former had nothing
as clothing to hide their shame except their two hands,
their long hair, or just closing of their eyes

यासां गोपाङ्गनानां लसदसिततरा लोललीलाकटाक्षा
यत्रासाचारुमुक्तामणिरुचिनिकरव्योमगंगाप्रवाहे ।
मीनायन्तेऽपि तासामतिरभसचलच्चारुनीलालकान्ता
भृङ्गायन्ते यदंघ्रिद्वयसरसिरुहे पातु पीतांबरो नः ॥

The playful glances of the belles of Vraja resemble the
fish in the flow of the celestial Ganga created by the
radiance of the pearls in the beautiful
nose-ornament of Krishna
The dark curly hair waving above their foreheads
looks like a swarm of bees when they
approach the lotus feet of Krishna
May that Krishna clothed in bright yellow
silks forever protect us!

CHAPTER VII

Kamadhenu

The cows and the calves follow Kaanha wherever he
goes and all of Gokula and Vrindavan love them as their
children, which is the reason Kamadhenu is revered as
the wish-fulfilling cow in mythology.

Kamadhenu

I AM A WARRIOR

According to the Puranas the earth-goddess was
originally in the form of a cow.

धेनूनामस्मि कामधुक् । धेनूनाम ॥

Among the cows I am Asmi
Lord Krishna reveals that among cows
He is manifested as Kamadhuk or Kamadhenu
The original wish-fulfilling cows
Also known as the Surabhi cows

I am Kamadhenu.

Most people view me as a cow but Hinduism describes
me as the divine bovine-goddess. In the literal sense I am the
cow of plenty or from whom all that is desired is drawn.

I am the owner of the eleven rudras and symbolised as
the wealth of the brahmana, the priest, and the sages and
there is a reason for this. My milk and its derivatives such as
ghee are integral parts of Vedic fire sacrifices, conducted by
priests.

In ancient India, I was also referred to Homadhenu, the cow from whom oblations are drawn.

I am the warrior and the protector of the priest who is prohibited by religion to engage in war or violence. In times of crisis and attack from kings, I create armies to protect my master and myself. That is why the priest reveres me as a goddess.

There are many stories about my origin.

Some believe I dwell in Goloka, the realm of cows, some say I descended from Patala, Netherworld. According to the Puranas the earth-goddess Prithvi was originally in the form of a cow, successively milked for beneficent substances by deities for the benefit of humans.

It is said that Prithu milked me to generate crops for human race to end a famine. That is how the word Kamadhenu, the miraculous "cow of plenty" and the "mother of cows" came about.

The Bhagavata Purana makes reference to me as Surabhi, a name given to me by Lord Krishna.

I am amongst the earliest animals on the planet.

I have witnessed what the Hindus describe Satyug as the golden age when India symbolised prosperity and abundance. I have experienced peace, divinity, and worship and this is because all the gods and the goddesses reside within me.

Legend says I emerged from the ocean of milk at the time of the Samudramanthana, churning of the ocean, by the gods and demons.

Legend says I was presented to the seven sages, and in the course of time, came into the custody of Sage Vashishta.

Legend also states that Lord Brahma created the cow and the priest at the same time so that both could aid each other in worship. The priests could recite scriptures while the cow would be productive in her offerings of clarified butter during the rituals.

I am Kamadhenu, symbol of the earth.

I represent life.

I am worshipped, garlanded on festivals. I am largely depicted as white cow with a female head and breasts.

Some say I am the daughter of Lord Daksha, some believe I am the wife of sage Kashyapa.

Some say I was in the possession of Sage Jamadagni and the enemy kings tried to steal me from him.

In the epic Ramayana, it is said that I was given as dowry to Goddess Sita when she married Lord Rama and I travelled with my siblings to her new home in Ayodhya.

In the Mahabharata, Bhishma Pitama declared me as the mother of the world.

There are so many tales, so many legends.

I am Asmita.

I am Kamadhenu.

It is said that I stood on my four feet in Satyug

Three feet in Tretayug

Two feet during the Dwaparyug

And only one leg during Kalyug.

Homadhenu

I AM THE BEHOLDER OF DEITIES
The scriptures link the anatomy of
the cow to the universe

गो अंगे यत लोमा तत सहस्र वत्सर ।
गो वधि राउरव मध्ये पेस् निरन्तर् ॥

Cow-killers and cow-eaters
Are condemned to rot in hell
For as many thousands of years
As the number of hair on the body
Of every cow they eat from

I am Nanda.

The scriptures describe my four legs as our Vedas; my nipples are the four purushartha: dharma-or righteousness, artha or material wealth, Kama or desire and moksha or salvation; my horns symbolise the gods, my face is chandra-surya, and my shoulders Agni, the god of fire.

I am Kamadhenu.

I have five other forms: Nanda, Sunanda, Surabhi, Susheela, and Sumana.

I am sacred, not just to the Hindus and to the Jains but other parts of the world like ancient Egypt, Palestine, and Rome.

The ancient Egyptians sacrificed animals but never sacrificed me and it is because I am sacred to goddess Hathor, who has the form of a cow.

In Egyptian mythology Hesat, a manifestation of Hathor is revered as the divine sky-cow in earthly form and Hathor is the wife of god Ra.

In the hieroglyphs the cow god is depicted wearing a hat.

I am a creation of intrigue and mystique.

I am a creation of story within stories.

It is believed that during the reign of King Vishwamitra, the kingdom was cursed with drought. The worried king went to Rishi Vashishta's ashram and pleaded for help. On arriving at his sacred dome, King Vishwamitra observed that Rishi Vashishta was praying to Kamadhenu Goddess, asking her to arrange food for all the guests accompanying the king.

Goddess Kamadhenu blessed all the guests with a delicious variety of food and drinks.

King Vishwamitra was stunned and turned greedy. He thought that if he could take Kamadhenu home then he and his kingdom would never fall short of food. He did not want to ask the sage for a favour and so tried to secretly steal Kamadhenu from the priest.

Rishi Vashishta noticed it and forbade him to do so. He advised the king that if he really wished to own Goddess Kamadhenu, he would have to do penance, he would have to become a saint by heart and soul, and that was not possible for the king.

King Vishwamitra could not possess me because I choose my master by his thoughts and deeds.

I am Sumana.

I am fortunate to have noble masters and knowledgeable caretakers who were sometimes sages, sometimes soldiers, and sometimes leaders.

In 1857, during the war when the soldiers discovered that the paper cartridges used contained gunpowder greased with cow and pig fat, the Hindu and the Muslim sepoys of the East India Company jointly protested against the abuse.

The Hindus worship me as the mother goddess, and so do the Muslims because eating suvar is forbidden in Islam. Both refused to bite off the end of the paper cartridge and the Britishers had to relent and think of an alternative.

Way before India's independence, the father of our nation Mahatma Gandhi said the central fact of Hinduism is my protection. He said I am more precious than the earthly mother because the earthly mother incurs expenses of burial or cremation while I am as useful dead as when alive.

I am Asmi, I am Ahi.

Our Puranas define me as the highest form of gift to mankind because I am the cow inside whom three hundred and thirty million deities reside.

Our ancestors held me on a pedestal, worshipped me as a deity, addressed me as mother but alas, not for long.

The first time, the human abused me and traded me; nature revolted and souls of higher attainment renounced the world.

Over a period of time, the human race lost interest in me and stopped reacting to my pain. I never thought it would happen but they turned cruel and insensitive.

With each passing year as the greed increased, the human lost his soul and quietly and shamelessly transformed from a sage into a beast.

In the Kalyug, he traded me, slaughtered me, and degraded me from a goddess to a commodity.

He forgot my essence, my identity. He forgot I was Kamadhenu, mother of cows.

He forgot the Vedas describing me as sacred somebody who cannot be harmed and killed.

With time, humans lost dignity and exchanged tradition for money.

He now tied bells on me everywhere and summoned me by any name and if I didn't listen, he whipped me with a stick.

Today, he trades every part of my body—my flesh, my bones, my intestines, my horns, and my skin. Today, I am not his mother but his property.

Once he could read my expressions and feel the pain in my eyes, now he has stopped looking into my eyes.

I am Nanda… and I am hardly visible today.

Sumana

I AM PANCHAGAVYA

The gift of cow is the highest and the most
supreme gift for mankind.

चिन्तामणि प्रकर सद्मसु कल्पवृक्श
लक्शवृतेषु सुरभीर अभिपालयन्तम् ।
लक्स्मी सहस्र सत सम्भ्रम सेव्यमानम्
गोविन्दमादिपुरुषं तमहं भजमि ॥

I worship Govinda, the primeval Lord
The progenitor who tends to cows
Surrounded by millions of purpose trees
Served with great reverence by both
Lakshmi and Gopi

I am Sunanda.

I am the supporter.

I am the provider.

For centuries the human race has survived on my dairy
products. For centuries, the kitchen fires have burned with
my offerings.

I have toiled, tilled and ploughed the farmer's fields. I have dragged and pulled his vendor's carts.

I have spread my dung on the village homes so that they kept warm.

I am fuel.

I am fertiliser.

For centuries my urine has been consumed in religious rituals and also used for medicinal purposes. The much talked about panchagavya is a mixture of my five products: my milk, my curds, my ghee, my urine and my dung.

I am disinfectant.

I am also the beast of burden.

I endured hardships for humans because they are my children. I believed this equation would never change but it is the law of nature that the new forgets the old and the human has forgotten their gau mata.

The universe regards human as its supreme creation because God imparted three special gifts to him, namely the heart, the mind, and the soul. But it seems as if he has lost touch with all three.

Over the centuries he disconnected with the virtues of life.

He disconnected with scriptures and Puranas.

He disconnected with rituals and religion.

He interfered with nature, with the cycle of birth and death.

He disrespects his ancestors and forgoes his tradition.

He neglected his gau mata and Nandi, my male

counterpart and loyal companion of Lord Shiva. Nandi is a symbol of respect for the male cattle and occupies the prime position outside Shiva temples at Thanjavur, Rameshwaram, and Mahabalipuram among the most venerated bovine shrines in the State of Tamil Nadu in Southern India.

You will never find a Shiva temple without Nandi and he is always seated facing the Lord. It is believed that if you tell your wish to Nandi, he will carry it to Lord Shiva because Nandi can reach Shiva where nobody else can.

Large numbers of pilgrims even today visit the sixteenth century Bull temple in Bangalore, Karnataka State and the eleventh century Nandi Temple at Khajuraho, Madhya Pradesh State. The Vishwanath Temple of Jhansi built in 1002 AD harbours a large bull worshipped for years.

I am Gau.

I am Paśu.

In the Hindu scriptures my calf is compared with dawn, the most auspicious time of the day when the sages rise to worship the deities.

The Rig Veda refers to me as Goddess and Nandi is referred to by the scriptures as the shadow of Lord Shiva.

Nandi is my consort and Nandini and Patti our daughters and both are worshipers of Lord Shiva.

The place where Patti submitted to Lord Shiva and attained salvation is known as Pattishwaram in Southern India and the river named after Nandini flowed with milk in Satyug and turned to water in Kalyug.

I am the milk cow.

I am Asaghyna.

I am mother.

I am Goddess.

～ VII.4 ～

Sunanda

I HAVE TRAVELLED FROM SATYUG TO KALYUG

In Vedas the cow is also known as
Asaghyna or inviolable.

सर्वे देवह् स्थित देहे सव देव मयीहि ।

All the deities

Dwell in the body of Kamadhenu

The Divine cow symbolises dharma

In Vedas the cow is also known as Asaghyna.

It means inviolable.

Ahi means not to be killed.

Aditi means not to be slaughtered.

I am Sunanda.

I have nine hundred twenty breeds and have travelled five thousand years. I am as old as the human being; in fact our forefathers commenced their journeys together. Human ancestors travelled to America as pilgrims accompanied by my forefathers and some of them settled down there and never came back.

Most of them did, which is why I'm well versed with all there is to know about the human race, their festivals, and their customs.

The human race brags about owning me but does it comprehend me, are they sensitive to what goes on in my heart and mind? I am not sure.

A human on an average lives up to eighty years and I can tell their age from their reflexes and their wrinkles. My breed lives for an average of eighteen years and a few of us, if we are fortunate, cross twenty-two to twenty-five years but is my master aware of this? Is he aware for instance that the way to gauge my age is not by my wrinkles but by counting the number of rings on my horn! Has my master in all these years taken the effort to investigate that and facilitate me accordingly? I don't think so.

Most of them know very little about our lineage and have little curiosity about our temperament or even biology. For instance I possess a total three-sixty-degree panoramic vision and I am able to detect all colours, except red and green. In a bullfight, it's not the red colour but the waving of the cape that provokes my male counterpart, the bull.

I can detect odours up to five miles away. I can hear lower and higher frequencies with precision.

I am Susheela.

I am trained to adapt into human routine, to adjust to his waking and sleeping patterns. I am a member of the family living in his cowshed, but is my master sensitised to my routine and requirements? Most of the time he discusses me with disdain to strangers in my very presence and I never reveal to him that I understand.

They haven't in all these centuries, understood that I require six hours to eat my food and another eight hours to chew the cud because it is our characteristic to chew minimum fifty times per minute. It is because I don't possess upper front teeth, which is the reason why I don't bite the grass—I just curl my tongue around it.

The human race eats and drinks as frequently as it desires, but does it make adequate provision of grain and water for me at all times? Most of the time they don't; my daily quota comprises thirty gallons of water and ninety-five pounds of feed per day. Does he make sure there is ample available in the cowshed for my friends and me?

He doesn't, which is why my friends and I are accustomed to remaining hungry all the time, accustomed to living each day as it comes.

We have slept hungry so many times, and woken up thirsty so many times because either the grain is insufficient or the water is preserved far away from our dwelling place and we were too weary to make the effort to walk that distance.

I stand on my feet all day but I am made to feel like I do nothing. Sometimes I stand longer hours because the master forgets to untie me from the cart and sometimes, he forgets to put me to sleep.

I pull his burden day after day yet once in a while, when I feel unwell, when my body temperature isn't 101.5 F and I need to rest, I am whipped and dragged out of my bed to get to daily work. He never misses an opportunity to refer to my weight, says it isn't easy to drag fourteen hundred pounds single-handedly.

Perhaps not.

Strange, he never finds my weight a problem when he exploits me for labour every day. It is never a problem when I carry his family and their luggage to their abode. Never a problem when he is collecting gallons of milk and the heavy weight of manure procured from me day after day and year after year.

I have accompanied him to various ceremonies, where he proudly proclaimes that I belong to him; I do, but I'm never treated as an equal. Each time he gets busy with the festivities and celebrations while I am relegated to a corner without food or a roof above me to protect from the sun.

The festivities go on for hours, sometimes till dusk while I'm standing.

After being with me for so many centuries, he still doesn't know that I don't like being alone. He does not know that I am as much of a social animal as him. I possess a heart too and it beats sixty and seventy beats per minute… and that, like him, I feel hurt when neglected and often weep silently when I am ignored.

He is so self absorbed he is most of the time indifferent to what I am thinking but I always know what he is thinking, what my friends are thinking, which is why you must have noticed we always travel in groups. We "moo" together when happy and peaceful and rest together when tired. We like company and abhor isolation.

Our masters don't know this because unlike other animals, we don't make eye contact yet; just from the body positions and facial expressions we are able to gauge what our companion is feeling...what our master is thinking.

Humans probably don't know this but we make friends and also foes.

I am Kamadhenu and I am proud of my large family.

✺ VII.5 ✺

Surabhi

I AM CREATED BY LORD KRISHNA

The spilt milk on the floor came to be recognised as the Kshirasagara or the Ocean of Milk.

नमो देव्यै महादेव्यै
सुरभ्यै च नमो नमःगवां बीज स्वरूपाय
नमस्ते जगदम्बिके ।

Kamadhenu
Is the desire-fulfilling cow of Heaven
Worshipping her
Along with her calf Nandini
Is auspicious
One who worships Kamadhenu
Is granted all desires
And blessings of
Goddesses Lakshmi, Durga and Saraswati
I am Surabhi, I am Manoratha...

Circumstances around me often dismay me but not for long. Deep within me I know that I am special and my self-worth comes from my Lord. I am his creation and as long as he believes in me I have nothing to fear. No master, no human, no circumstances can cause me harm because I am protected by the Parakrami himself!

Lord Gopala is my cowherd, my protector, and my caretaker. He represents dharma and as long as he is beside me no evil can befall me.

I am privileged that the Puranas link me to customs and festivals associated with Lord Krishna.

In South India and some parts of Sri Lanka, a cattle festival called Maattu Pongal is celebrated and this marks the beginning of the harvest time.

Among the innumerable stories about my origin, my favourite is the story of Devi Bhagavata Purana. It says that

Lord Krishna and his beloved Radha were one day, relaxing in the company of each other far away in the meadows, when they suddenly felt extremely thirsty.

There was no spring or pond in sight and so Krishna, to quench his beloved's thirst, created a cow, Surabhi, and a calf, Manoratha, from the left side of his body, which is why the left side of Krishna's body is referred to as the female side of the deity.

It is said that Krishna first offered his prayers to Kamadhenu and then ordained that she would henceforth be revered as the symbol of prosperity and worshipped on the festival of Diwali.

Krishna then milked the cow, transferred it to a pot and was proceeding to drink it when the earthen pot slipped from his hands and fell to the ground and broke! The spilt milk on the floor came to be recognised as the Kshirasagara or the Ocean of Milk.

Several cows miraculously emerged from Surabhi created by Lord Krishna and he distributed them among gopas, his shepherd-friends, requesting them to look after them as their babies.

Lord Krishna was called Gopala when he was a child and Gopala means the protector of cows. There are many esoteric meanings to the word Gopala, and all of them symbolise spiritual beauty. It is said that Gopala was such a lovable baby that all the gopis in the neighbouring villages loved him more than their children.

Not only that, all the cows in the vicinity loved Gopala

more than they loved their own calves and this is evident in all the old and new posters portraying Lord Krishna playing the flute to gau Kamadhenu and calf Manoratha.

The Brahmakumaris have a unique and contemporary interpretation of Krishna and his cow. They believe that Krishna's flute is an awakening from Shivbaba, an avatar of Lord Krishna to enlighten mankind from ignorance. They believe it is to motivate followers to the murli of knowledge. The flute is a process of rising from the body-consciousness to the soul-consciousness.

According to the Brahmakumaris Raj Yog, Shivbaba often described his dwelling place as a gaushala and the Brahmakumaris as his cows. The Kamadhenu is a path of bhakti. The milk overflowing from the earthen pot is symbolic of knowledge in the same way as the urn of amrit is symbolic of enlightenment and also the reason the pot slipped from the hands of Sri Krishna because knowledge is to be shared not restricted. The beauty about legends is that they are open to interpretations.

There is another story, about what followed after Krishna held up the Govardhan Mountain on his little finger.

It is said that Lord Indra visited him to seek mercy for his wrong deeds. He pleaded with Krishna to become the saviour of the cows and the sages and promised him that all cows idolising Brahma will perform abhisheka ritual in his honour.

Lord Indra kept his word.

I know the story because I have been a witness to the dialogue and participated in the abhisheka performed by Lord Indra and his elephant Airavata.

The abhisheka was a moment to remember when we honoured Sri Krishna with the name of "Govinda."

It was a day-long celebration when the universe was filled with joy and fragrance.

I am Surabhi.

I am special because I am Sri Krishna's creation.

सरसगुणनिकायं सच्चिदानन्दकायं
शमितसकलमायं सत्यलक्ष्मीसहायम् ।
शमदमसमुदायं शान्तसर्वान्तरायं
सुहृदयजनदायं नौमि गोपालराजम् ॥

**I bow to the king of cowherds who is the
repository of all good qualities
Who is the embodiment of absolute truth,
of awareness and bliss!
Who removes all delusions, who is the
consort of Lakshmi
Who has conquered his senses and mind,
who has surmounted all obstacles
And who is the friend of the large-hearted
and noblemen**

लक्ष्मीकलत्रं ललिताब्जनेत्रं
पूर्णेन्दवक्त्रं पुरुहूतमित्रम् ।
कारुण्यपात्रं कमनीयगात्रं
वन्दे पवित्रं वसुदेवपुत्रं ॥

I bow to the son of Vasudeva, who is pure,
who is the consort of Lakshmi
Who has beautiful lotus-like eyes, whose face is like the
full moon, who is the friend of Indra, who is full of mercy
and who has a handsome body

मदमयमदमयदुरगं
यमुनामवतीर्य वीर्यशालि यः ।
मम रतिममरतिरस्कृति-
शमनपरस्स क्रियात् कृष्णः ॥

May that Krishna create in me endless
devotion towards Him
Krishna who dived into river Yamuna and valiantly
subjugated the aggressive snake Kaliya
And who removes the misfortunes of the celestials

CHAPTER VIII

Shankha

When Kaanha departs from Gokula to meet King Kamsa
in Mathura, Radha snatches his bansuri from him in the hope
that he would return to Vrindavan to get his flute from her.
He never does and after he turns an emperor, the conch
replaces the flute in his life.

Shankha

I AM PART OF PRAYER AND WORSHIP
I disperse negative energy and spread positivity.

सशङ्खचक्रं सकिरीटकुण्डलं सपीतवस्त्रं सरसीरुहेक्षणम् ।
सहारवक्षस्थलशोभिकौस्तुभं नमामि विष्णुं शिरसा चतुर्भुजम् ॥

Salutations to Sri Vishnu holding the shankha
and chakra in his hands
Who is adorned with shining earrings,
dressed in yellow garments
He bestows grace with his lotus-like eyes
His chest adorned with a garland clipped with the
Kaustubha gem; I bow my head before Lord Vishnu

I am Shankha.

I am oblong in shape. I have a protuberance in the middle, but taper at the two ends. My upper portion known as the thesiphonal canal is corkscrew-shaped, while the lower end, the spire is twisted and tapering.

I am dull in colour and my surface is brittle and translucent. Like all snail shells, my inside is hollow. I am made from the species Turbinella Pyrum, from the Indian

185

Ocean. I am decorated with ornate patterns in metals such as silver, bronze, and tin, topped with a bright bead, the source of all positive energy.

I was originally used as a war trumpet. Kings and warriors declared war open blowing my trumpet on the battle field and closed war at sunset with my trumpet again.

I am identified with the deities. Seers believe that I am blown to invoke Lord Shiva and there is a special connection between us which is evident from the similarity in our names.

I am Shankara.

I am associated with Lord Shiva.

I am associated with Lord Vishnu.

I am the abode of Goddess Lakshmi, who is the goddess of wealth and consort of Vishnu and because I emerge from the water, I am also regarded as a symbol of female fertility and associated with serpents.

I am part of the scriptures; part of ancient art forms. All classical dance forms have mudras devoted to me. I am part of ancient philosophy.

Our ancestors believe that one who preserves me is God's chosen one and blessed with fame and longevity.

There is an old belief that a cracked conch should not be preserved in a temple or home; however if the cracked part is mounted in gold or silver my virtues are restored.

I am identified by my unique and reverberating sound associated with the sacred and the first sound of creation, Om.

I am also associated with royalty, with the Indian princely state of Travancore, and the Kingdom of Cochin.

I am one of the eight auspicious symbols of Buddhism and the Ashtamangala, the proud emblem of the Indian state of Kerala.

Few people know that there are two types of me: Dakshinavarta shankha and Vamavarta shankha differentiated from the direction of my coiling.

A Dakshinavarta shankha is the very rare sinistral form of the species, where the shell coils or whorls expand in a counter clockwise spiral if viewed from the apex of my shell.

The second, Vamavarta shankha is the very commonly occurring dextral form of the species, where the shell coils or whorls expand in a clockwise spiral when viewed from the apex of my shell.

In Hinduism, a Dakshinavarta shankha symbolises infinite space and is associated with Lord Vishnu while the Vamavarta shankha represents the reversal of the laws of nature and is linked with Lord Shiva.

The Dakshinavarta shankha is the abode of the wealth goddess Lakshmi—the consort of Vishnu, and therefore utilised for medicinal purposes.

The right spiral reflects the motion of the universal planets and is associated with the hair whorls on Lord Buddha's crown that spiral to the right. The long white curl between Buddha's eyebrows and the conch-like swirl of his navel are often compared to my pure white form.

The Varaha Purana mentions that bathing with the

Dakshinavarta shankha frees human being from suffering and sin.

The Skanda Purana narrates that bathing Lord Vishnu with Dakshinavarta shankha frees you from sins of seven previous lives.

A Dakshinavarta shankha is preserved as a rare jewel and it is believed that worshipping it results in being blessed with virtues.

There is an oft-repeated story about me; the story of the biggest battle between the good versus the evil. So when the final cry of victory went up from the Gods, everyone was relieved that their deadliest enemy was slain and Lord Shiva took up Sankhachuda's bones and flung them into the ocean.

He said, these bones shall become the sacred conch shells used in worship everywhere and ever since it is believed that wherever and whenever I am blown, Goddess Lakshmi makes it a point to dwell inside me which is why the water inside me is regarded as sacred as the holy river and can be offered to all the demigods except to Lord Shiva because he is the vanquisher!

I am the forbearer of a legacy. I am blessed and also the cursed.

Blessed because Goddess Lakshmi resides within me and cursed because Radha Rani accuses me of stealing her Kaanha away from her.

The bansuri looks on me as her rival because as long as Kaanha was in Gokula, the flute was forever on his lips or tied onto his waist band.

All of Vrindavan, the gopalas and the gopis are annoyed with me because they feel I have snatched their friend away from them.

How do I explain to them that it is my Lord who comes in search of me and not the other way round? How do I tell them that He dictates the time and the tenure, the exile and the attachment? In Gokula it was the flute, in Dwarka it is me, the conch and later, after the Yadav yatra it will be the Peepala tree.

All of us have our roles to play in his journey and when the time is up, he moves on.

∽ VIII.2 ∾

Shankara

I AM THE WIND INSTRUMENT
I am decorated with ornate patterns in metals.
Let us sing the praises of Lord Vishnu.

सशङ्खचक्रं सकिरीटकुण्डलं सपीतवस्त्रं सरसीरुहेक्षणम् ।
सहारवक्षस्थलशोभिकौस्तुभं नमामि विष्णुं शिरसा चतुर्भुजम् ॥

He who holds the conch, the spinning discus
and is adorned with earrings
Let us sing praises of the yellow-clothed, one who

**is the Lord of the serpents
Apart from many kinds of weapons, Lord Krishna
bears the Kaustubha mani on his chest
Let us bow before the four-armed Vishnu
and seek his blessings**

I am Shankara.

I am the wind instrument.

Like the flute, I had to endure pain before I was created. A hole is drilled near the tip of my apex so when air is blown through this hole, it travels through the whorls of the shankha, producing a loud, sharp, shrill sound called Shakhand.

This sound is the reason why I was chosen as a war trumpet, I am loud and clear enough to be heard by the warriors on the battle front, to summon help for the wounded on a barren land far away.

For a long time I only travelled to the battlefield, watched the soldiers bleed and put up a brave fight with their enemies. For a long time I only heard the swords and cries of pain and looked forward to sunset so that the warriors could throw their weapons and nurse their wounds and I wondered how long I would suffer this agony of watching hatred and revenge.

The universe heard my plea and gradually as the emperors faded and the wars diminished I was exited from the battlefield and put in a place of worship. I don't know who thought about this and why but I will always be grateful. I had thought I would return to the ocean but some wise man decided my sound is auspicious and should be preserved in the house.

I was allotted the place of worship; it is my good fortune my Lord that I was put at your feet. I loved my new surroundings; I loved the fragrance and the tranquillity. After being amidst bloodshed for so many years it was calming to be around so much love and devotion. On the battle field I was in the care of the senapati, now I was the custodian of the woman of the house. Every morning, fresh after a shower, she would wake me up and the other deities in her temple. She would sprinkle rose water, some kumkum, some flowers and after bowing to all, blow me loud and strong.

She was so gentle, so caring, picked me up and placed me back in my position so carefully as to not hurt or scar me with a single blemish. I was part of her everyday prayers, part of her daily prayer to the cosmos.

Our sunrise and sunset relationship has lasted many generations; we have together spread good will and harmony for everyone around us. It is my honour that I am utilised to bathe idols of deities, especially Lord Vishnu and care has to be exercised that no hole is drilled in my apex.

I am also used as a container to preserve holy water.

I am worship.

Bathing by the waters led through me, a shankha, is equivalent to bathing in holy water.

Shankha Sadma Purana declares that bathing an image of Vishnu with cow milk is as virtuous as performing a million yajnas, and bathing Vishnu with Ganges river water frees one from the cycle of births.

The mere sight of me dispels all sins just as the Sun God dispels the fog.

The mere sound of me dispels all negative vibrations.

Just seeing me…

Just having me in the home…

is auspicious.

In Buddhism, the conch shell has been incorporated as one of the eight auspicious symbols, also called ashtamangala.

In Hinduism, there is the image of Matsya, fish avatar of Vishnu, holding me in his right lower hand: He kills a demon called Shankhasura, who emerges from another shankha.

I am part of Vishnu.

Whether sitting or standing Lord Vishnu is always depicted holding me in his left upper hand. The Sudarshana Chakra, Gada and Padma decorate his upper right, the lower left, and lower right hand, respectively. All avatars of Krishna, Kurma, Varaha, and Narasimha hold me with love and care and when he holds me in his avatar of Vishnu, I am bestowed a new name.

I become Panchajanya.

I am Sunga.

Besides Lord Vishnu, other deities also carry me in their hands; the sun god Lord Surya, the king of Heaven Lord

Indra, the war god Lord Kartikeya, Goddess Vaishnavi, Goddess Durga and Gaja Lakshmi.

Sometimes, I am personified as ayudhapurusha weapon-man in the sculpture and depicted as a man standing beside Vishnu or his avatars. This subordinate figure is called the Shankhapurusha who is depicted holding a shankha in both the hands.

I am Shankara…I am evident everywhere in the temples…On the pillars, on the temple walls, on the temple gopuras. The city of Puri where Lord Jagannath resides is celebrated and recognised as shankha-kshetra. I am also connected to Shaligrama, another form of Lord Vishnu.

Shaligrama stones are usually found in the Gandaki River in Nepal are worshipped by Hindus as a representative of Vishnu.

The way to recognise a Shaligrama is it has marks of shankha, chakra, gada, and padma arranged in this particular order and which is why Shaligrama is seen as an avatar of Keshava.

There are twenty-four orders of the four symbols defined for Shaligrama and the same for worship of Lord Vishnu in different names: Madhusudana, Damodara, Balarama, and Vamana.

Sri Krishna promised Tulsi that he would descend from the Heaven on earth one day in a year to marry her. This day is celebrated as Tulsi vivaah and falls a fortnight after the festival of Diwali.

Prajanya

I EMERGED DURING THE CHURNING OF THE OCEAN

I have many forms, many names.

त्रैलोक्ये यानि तीर्थानि वासुदेवस्य चाज्ञया ।
शङ्खे तिष्ठन्ति विपेन्द्र तस्माद शङ्खं प्रपूजयेत् ॥
त्वं पूरा सागरोत्पन्नः विष्णुना विधृतः करे ।
निर्मितः सर्वदेवैस्तु पाञ्चजन्य नमोऽस्तुते ॥

**Whatever tirthas are there in the three Worlds,
by the command of Vasudeva,
they abide inside the Shankha. O best of Wise men,
thus Shankha is to be worshipped,
In former times You rose from the Sea and
Vishnu held you in his hand,
You are worshipped by all the devas; salutations
to Panchajanya.**

I am Prajanya

There is an interesting story about how I was created

According to Brahma Vaivarta Purana, Lord Shiva flung

a trident towards the asuras and they were demolished

194

instantly. Their ashes flew into the sea and transformed into conches.

According to our ancient scriptures or Puranas, I emerged during the churning of the ocean and the deities preserved me in the form of a weapon.

A holy verse which is regularly chanted during a ritual of worship says: By the command of Lord Vishnu, Lord Chandra, Surya, and Varuna reside inside me.

Lord Prajapati resides on my surface and pilgrimages like River Ganga and River Saraswati are on my front, which is why the vibrations emanating from me are so powerful.

Lord Vishnu is associated with his four aayudh weapons: the Sudarshana Chakra, the Kaumodakee gada, the lotus and me, Panchajanya shankha. Legend also has it that an asura by the name of Shankhasura was demolished by Matsya, the fish avatar of Lord Vishnu.

I am the lucky one to have been a witness to both the Mahabharata and to the Ramayana and let me share that brothers Lakshmana, Bharata and Shatrughna are incarnations of Sheshnaag, Sudarshana Chakra and the Shankha. Lord Rama, as everyone knows, is one of the ten avatars of Lord Vishnu. Krishna, as the charioteer of Arjuna, blew me at the Kurukshetra battle front in the eighteenth or the nineteenth century.

Goddess Lakshmi was discovered during amritmanthan from the sea, so in that sense she is my soul sister.

I am Panchajanya.

In Sanskrit, Panchajanya means having control over the

five classes of beings. The Pandava brothers Yudhishthira, Bhima, Arjuna, Nakula, and Sahadeva are described to possess shankhas named Ananta-Vijaya, Poundra-Khadga, Devadatta, Sughosha, and Mani-pushpaka.

A legend states that while using me as a part of a meditative ritual, a sadhu blew me facing the direction of Keoli village and a snake crept out of the forest. The snake advised the sadhu to worship me as Nāga Devata and since then the tradition continues.

I am Shanku Naga.

I have many forms, many names.

Some know me as the Gaumukhi shankha, some as Ganesha shankha, some as Kauri shankha, Moti shankha and some others as Heera shankha.

I represent one hundred zillion in number…I am one of the nine treasures of Lord Kuber, the God of wealth. His attendant, Shanknidhi, a corpulent dwarf seated in an easy posture always holds me in his hand.

Shankhnidhi has an identical looking companion, Padmanidhi and the only way to tell the difference is that while Shankhnidhi holds me, his companion holds a lotus in his hand.

I am auspicious, but guided by rules.

If I am used as part of worship in a temple I cannot be used as a trumpet on the battlefront. Blowing me has a special significance and has to be adhered as per Varaha Purana.

The temple door where I reside, for instance, can only be opened after blowing me. To commence the devotion I have to be blown from my left side in three frequencies: The first, sattva dominant, second, raja dominant and finally tama dominant.

The sattva dominant frequencies get attracted to the place of ritual but are opposed by the raja and the tama dominant frequencies.

My energy however demolishes all distressing frequencies and forms armour of chaitanya, a divine consciousness conducive to worship.

There is another advantage. Every time I am blown Lord Vishnu is drawn to the venue.

The appropriate way to use me is to first raise your neck and bend it backwards. Then, take a deep breath and begin to blow with increasing intensity.

I have to be consumed in one single breath and if this is done in the right way, I activate the Sushumna channel and this automatically strikes a balance that is positive for the worshipper and eliminates negative energies surrounding the place.

I am Shankha.

Like the bansuri I have been physically closest to my Lord.

VIII.4

Chanku

I AM APPRECIATED IN BUDDHISM
My shells are regarded as symbols of love and marriage.

पवनाय नमः
पाञ्चजन्याय नमः
पद्मगर्भाय नमः
अम्बुराजाय नमः
कंबुराजाय नमः
धवलाय नमः
पाञ्चजन्याय विद्महे पद्मगर्भाय धीमहि तन्त्रः शङ्खः प्रचोदयात् ॥

**Om, Let us contemplate on Panchajanya shankha of
Sri Krishna and meditate on Pavamana,
May that Shankha awaken our consciousness**

I am chanku.

In the Western world, in the English language, I am known as the conch.

I am found in the Gulf of Mannar, Gulf of Khambat, and also near the mouth of the Narmada River.

I am as appreciated in Buddhism as in Hinduism.

In ancient Greece, I am considered as symbol of mother

goddesses. My shells, along with pearls, are considered symbols of sexual love and everlasting marriage.

There is an intricate and elaborate process of how I have to participate in a ritual.

The pointed side of me is placed directed toward the deity. This way the house of worship is blessed with positive energy. I have to be filled with water prior to the actual puja of a deity and followed by the kalash puja. The seers in the olden days dressed me in sandalwood paste, flowers, and Tulsi leaves.

When my worship ends, the devotee sprinkles the water filled inside me on the deity and the articles used in the ritual. This water is as pure as the water from the Ganga River and used for bathing the deities.

I am shankha.

I am custom.

My female part is called shankhini.

Shankhini is rough and thorny and does not emanate a pleasant sound and therefore considered inauspicious for a place of worship. Only tantriks following the Aghori Vidya to accumulate black energy use Shankhini considered inauspicious by everyone else.

I am medicine.

Ancient science used my shell ash described in Sanskrit as shankha bhasma, to cure all kinds of ailments. In those days I was soaked in lime juice and calcinated in covered crucibles innumerable times and reduced to powder ash.

I contain calcium, iron, and magnesium which make me antacid and cure all digestive problems.

My ash mixed with tamarind seed ash, five salts, asafoetida, ammonium chloride, pepper, carui, caraway, ginger, long pepper, purified mercury, and aconite in specified proportions, triturated in juices of lemon and is prescribed for wind, air and bile ailments, as well as for beauty and strength.

I am as popular in Ayurveda medicine as in prayer and worship. A powder made out of my ingredients is a cure for stomach ailments and beneficial to building strength.

Simply by seeing me
Simply by touching
Simply by remembering
Simply by listening to me
Or having me around
…there is auspiciousness.
I am senkhu.
I am sankham.
I am sankha.
I am shankho.

त्वय्यप्रसन्ने मम किं गुणेन ।
रक्ते विरक्ते च वरे वधूनां
निरर्थकः कुङ्कुमपत्रभंगः ॥

O Lord! When you are pleased what is the
use of good qualities in me?
If you are not pleased, then also what is the
use of good qualities in me?
If the groom loves her, the bride need
not adorn herself with Kumkumapatra
If he does not love her, then also
the Kumkumapatra is useless

गायन्ति क्षणदावसानसमये सानन्दमिन्दप्रभां
रुन्धन्त्यो निजदन्तकान्तिनिवहैर्गोपाङ्गना गोकुले ।
मथ्नन्त्यो दधि पाणिकङ्कणझणत्कारानुकारं जवा-
द्यावद्द्वसनाञ्चला यमनिशं पीतांबरोऽव्यात्स नः ॥

When the night ends and the morning breaks the gopis
of Gokula joyfully sing the praises of Krishna blocking
the moon with the brilliance of his white teeth
They sing the praises of Krishna, churning curds as their
jingling bracelets create music and their
saris flutter in the wind
May that Krishna who clothes himself in bright yellow
silks protect us now and forever!

मल्लैः शैलेन्द्रकल्पः शिशुरितरजनैः पुष्पचापोऽङ्गनाभिः
गोपैस्तु प्राकृतात्मा दिवि कुलिशभृता विश्वकायोऽप्रमेयः ।
क्रुद्धः कंसेन कालो भयचकितदृशा योगिभिर्ध्येयमूर्तिः
दृष्टो रंगावतारे हरिरमरगणानन्दकृत्पातु युष्मान् ॥

When Krishna entered the stage at the Dhanuryagna of
Kamsa, the wrestlers saw him as a big mountain
Ordinary people saw him as a child,
women saw him as the god of Love
The cowherds saw him as an ordinary person
Lord Indra in Heaven saw him as the cosmic
power beyond measurement
Kamsa, his uncle with terror in his eyes,
saw him as furious Death
Yogis saw him as one who is to be meditated upon
May that Hari who delights the celestials protect
us time and again!

CHAPTER IX

Peepala Tree

Lord Krishna breathes his last sitting beneath the Peepala tree, ever since regarded as a tree of worship in Hindu religion. He returns from the Yadav yatra when a tribal, mistaking him for a beast, shoots an arrow into his foot.

Peepala

I AM THE KING OF TREES

The Peepala tree houses the Trimurti, the roots being
Brahma, the trunk Vishnu and the leaves, Shiva

Bhagavad Gita Chapter 15.1

श्रीभगवानुवाच ।
ऊर्ध्वमूलमध:शाखमश्वत्थं प्राहुरव्ययम् ।
छन्दांसि यस्य पर्णानि यस्तं वेद स वेदवित् ॥

The Supreme Personality of Godhead said:
It is believed that there is an imperishable
Peepala tree That has its roots upward and
its branches falling on the floor
It is believed that these leaves are the Vedic hymns
And one who is familiar with the Peepala tree
Is the knower of the Vedas!

I am Peepala.

In the Bhagavad Gita Lord Krishna says, among the
trees I am Ashwatha. I am the beholder of the Trimurti.

Lord Brahma is my roots. Lord Vishnu my trunk and Lord Shiva my leaves.

There is an ancient story how this happened, a story as old as the hills.

The gods chose to hold their councils under the shade of my branches and that is how I came to be associated with spiritual understanding.

The Brahma Purana and the Padma Purana relate another equally delightful story about an ongoing fight between the demons and the deities when Lord Vishnu sought refuge inside me to escape a particularly dangerous demon.

Legend has it that Lord Vishnu dwelled inside me for a long, long time until the demons stopped hunting for him and which is why devotees of Vishnu hold me in high esteem.

There is another story connected to Vishnu's consort Goddess Lakshmi. The belief is that Goddess Lakshmi was worried about her husband's long absence from home and came searching for him. When she discovered that Vishnu inhabited inside me, she insisted on joining him as well and now that both were together, they relished their stay and their tranqulity spread fragrance all around.

Soon the birds, the bees, the insects and the passing animals were drawn to their aroma and stopped beneath my shade to rest for a while. The humans wondered what was so special about me that everyone appeared so calm just being around me. Slowly, they began frequenting me too and over the years marked a special day of the week to celebrate me and the tradition has continued for generations. They consider it auspicious to worship me on Saturday because they are convinced it is the day both Vishnu and Lakshmi reside inside me even today.

In the month of Shravan if an unmarried woman ties a red thread around me, circumambulates sprinkling water and flowers, I am indebted to fulfil her desire for a suitable husband. I am indebted to grant a son to a married woman praying for a child too.

I am worship.

I am a boon.

The Skanda Purana considers me a symbol of worship and professes that if a family without an heir serves and regards me as son, I will carry forward the family legacy for as long as I live.

The Upanishads refer to me as a metaphor to explain the relevance of the body and the soul: the body is the fruit which we see outside while the soul is the seed, invisible and internal.

There is a third story popularised by the Brahma Purana, which tells about two daring demons, Ashwatha and Peepala. It is said that Ashvatha would take the form of a Peepala and Peepala would take the form of a brahmana and they harassed voyagers who passed their path. Peepala, in the form of a fake brahmana would advise people to touch Ashwatha and seek blessings, and when they did, Ashwatha would kill them!

They played this nasty trick on people for many years until they were punished by a very angry Lord Shani Maharaj which explains why Lord Shani has come to be associated with me as well. Initially I was exploited to drive away Lord Shani but I decided to befriended him instead and today we are an extension of each other.

It is beneath my shade that centuries ago, Goddess Sita took refuge in Lanka and Lord Hanuman visited her carrying the ring of Lord Rama.

I have witnessed the birth of Vishnu.

The final journey, samadhi of Sri Krishna, after a hunter called Zaara, mistaking him for a deer, shot him with an arrow.

I am as old as the deities.

I have been watching over the universe since Mohenjo-daro, one of the cities of the Indus Valley Civilization of 3000 BC—1700 BC and that is probably the reason why cutting me is considered 'Panchapataka' among the five deadly sins in Hindu religion, equivalent to killing a brahmana.

I am ancient.

I am tradition.

I am Arasu.

Ashwatha

I AM IMPERISHABLE

The roots go down reflecting the furtive actions
of human society.

Bhagavad Gita: Chapter 15.2,

अधश्चोर्ध्वं प्रसृतास्तस्य शाखा
गुणप्रवृद्धा विषयप्रवाला: ।
अधश्च मूलान्यनुसन्ततानि
कर्मानुबन्धीनि मनुष्यलोके ॥

**The branches of this tree extend downward and upward,
nourished by the three modes of material nature.
The twigs are the objects of the senses.**

This tree also has roots going down, and these are bound
to the furtive actions of human society.

I am Ashwatha.

In Tamil Nadu they call me Arasan which literally means
the king of trees. In Andhra Pradesh I am Raavi Chettu. In
Kerala I am Aarayaal and in Karnataka I am Aralimara. In
different regions of different countries I have different names.

I am recognised as Ficus Religiosa in other parts of the universe, referred to as the Bodhi tree by followers of Buddhist faith, as it was beneath me that Lord Buddha found enlightenment.

I have multiple names but I am usually recognised by my shape and size. I am large; my bark is grey, peeled in patches. My leaves are heart-shaped with tapering tips and my fruit is purple when ripe. The slightest breeze makes me rustle.

Some say the rustling is a result of Sri Krishna residing in me but more about this later.

I am divine.

I am intriguing.

I am robust.

I am tradition.

My roots are firm and my direction unchangeable.

I am planted to the east of the house or the temple and if faced in another direction, I refuse to grow. There are customs associated with me and those housing me have to follow these rituals.

I am the first-known depicted tree in India.

I am as ancient as the Mohenjo-daro civilisation.

I have been watching the universe for centuries.

I am Plaska.

When I turn twelve and enter puberty, the temple purohit or the Karta of the family performs the Upanayan ceremony. This entails building of a circular platform around me and invoking Lord Narayana, Lord Vasudeva and Goddesses Rukmini and Satyabhama.

The Neem tree is always planted beside me in a way our branches intermingle as we grow taller. On Amavasya night, many villagers perform a symbolic marriage between us. The Neem represents the Shivalinga while I, the Peepala, represent the yoni, power of the female.

During the marriage ceremony performed between the two trees, the fruit of the Neem is placed on a Peepala leaf to depict the Shivalinga, which symbolises creation through sexual union, after which the two trees are considered "married." After the ceremony, the villagers circle the trees to express happiness and to seek their blessings and to get rid of their sins.

In ancient times, the grower of both these trees also adopted a snake—real or idol—and placed it between the two trees. It is believed that the worshipper of the snake is blessed with wealth and fortune. These practices, though not prescribed by any religious texts, are followed by many even today.

Ayurveda Science regards me as a medicine and has proved that my bark is used to yield tannin; my leaves, when heated, are useful in treating stubborn wounds.

Modern science says that movement is life and life is oxygen. Unlike other trees that blossom during specific seasons, I stand tall and green all through the year. I release oxygen all the time, day and night, which is why people usually feel better, seated beneath my shade.

I told you that my leaves flutter because Sri Krishna resides inside me and that is not the only fable. There are many theories elaborating this phenomenon. The Hindus attribute it to the ancestors who dwell inside me and continuously flutter to make us aware of their presence. This is also the reason why people bow their heads when they pass my sight. My rustling leaves have a mention in the Bhagavad Gita when Sri Krishna says, "O Ashwatha, I honour you whose leaves are forever fluttering."

Sri Krishna, in another verse of the Bhagavad Gita, says, "I am Narada among the sages, Chitraratha among the Gandharvas, sage Kapila among the Siddhas and Peepala among the trees."

Is it surprising then that ascetics even today, meditate beneath the sacred fig tree believed to be guarded by the twenty-seven constellations, constituting twelve houses and nine planets, specifically represented by twenty-seven trees?

I am blessed by the cosmos.

I am Arasan.

I am Aarayaal.

~ IX.3 ~

Arayal

I AM MYTH, ALSO MEDICINE

Bhagavad Gita: Chapter 15.3 & .4

न रूपमस्येह तथोपलभ्यते
नान्तो न चादिर्न च सम्प्रतिष्ठा ।
अश्वत्थमेनं सुविरूढमूल
मसङ्गशस्त्रेण दृढेन छित्वा ॥
ततः पदं तत्परिमार्गितव्यं
यस्मिन्गता न निवर्तन्ति भूयः ।
तमेव चाद्यं पुरुषं प्रपद्ये
यतः प्रवृत्तिः प्रसृता पुराणी ॥

**The real form of this tree cannot be
perceived in this world
No one can understand where it ends, where it
begins, or where its foundation is
With determination one must cut down this strong tree
with the weapon of detachment
Thereafter, seek the place where having
gone one never returns
And there, surrender to that Supreme**

Personality of Godhead
From whom everything began and from whom everything has extended since time immemorial

I am Aralimara.

The brahmanas associate me with river Saraswati rising from the water pot of Brahma in the Himalayas.

The tribals in Bengal address me as Vasudeva and water me in the month of Vaishakh.

Parents who face difficulty marrying their daughters of age marry them to me and all of them soon find suitable grooms. In olden days, when remarriage was forbidden for widows, they were married to me and then allowed to remarry.

In many communities a marriage ceremony is not complete without a branch of my tree. The branch, along with a pot of water, is placed between the bride and the groom while the pundit chants the mantras. The presence of a Peepala leaf assures a happy and secure marriage because it has the blessings of Lord Vishnu and Goddess Lakshmi.

In contemporary times I am the shade where the Panchayat assembles to grant justice to the villagers...

It is said that the original tree in Bodhgaya Bihar was destroyed and replaced several times over. Apparently a branch of the original tree was rooted in Anuradhapura, Sri Lanka in 288 BCE which is even today, revered as Jaya Sri Maha Bodhi, the oldest flowering plant in the world.

In Theravada Buddhist Southeast Asia, the residents worship the massive trunk as a shrine.

I am Peepdo.

I have both mythological and medical significance.

If dried in the sun and my powder consumed with a pinch of jaggery and water, I serve as a laxative. In case of dysentery just chew my leaves with coriander and sugar and the stomach will return to normal.

I am effective in treating heart disorders. I serve as a tonic for the body, cure skin disorders and if suffering from jaundice, I am the fastest and the easiest cure.

I am a cure for mumps, for boils, and for swellings. I dissolve infection; dissolve bacteria and even speech disorders. It has been proven that if you lick honey placed on my leaf, speech irregularities will be resolved forever.

I am a native of India and thrive in hot, humid climate. I grow inside the house but the best place to plant me is outside home where I can embrace the sky and talk to sunlight, smile at the moon and sing with the clouds.

Sages over the years have perceived me in different forms. Seer Shankaracharya interprets me as "One which does not remain the same tomorrow." There is a reason why he describes me so.

It is said that once, all the gods decided to visit Lord Shiva impromptu and Lord Narada warned them not to, because that was the time Lord Shiva and Goddess Parvati were in solitude. But Lord Indra was adamant and did not pay heed to Narada's advice. Lord Narada was forced to announce their arrival and as predicted, Goddess Parvati disapproved of the invasion and cursed that all the deities be transformed into trees.

The Gods realised their folly and pleaded forgiveness. By this time Goddess Parvati had also calmed down, but what had been done could not be undone so Parvati modified her curse that the deities, while in the form of trees, will serve the universe.

Thus Lord Indra transformed into a Mango tree, Lord Brahma into a Palash tree and Lord Vishnu into a Peepala tree.

Another equally compelling story is about Lord Agni who, one day, for reasons unknown descended from heaven and adapted the form of Ashwatha and resided on top of me for a long, long time refusing to return to paradise.

Since then, Peepala is also known as Ashwatha.

I am Ashwatha.

I am custom.

I am ritual.

I am the king of trees!

दृष्टिः संवलिता रुचा कुचयुगे स्वर्णप्रभे श्रीमति ।
बालः कश्चन चूतपल्लव इति प्रान्तस्मितास्यश्रियं
श्लिष्यंस्तामथ रुक्मिणीं नतमुखीं कृष्णः
स पुष्णातु नः ॥

When Krishna pulled her upper garment,
Rukmini shyly cast her eyes down
The dark lashes drooping over her large
breasts lit up her face in a golden hue
Krishna embraced Rukmini and she bowed to
him like a blooming leaf of the mango tree

उर्व्यां कोऽपि महीधरो लघुतरो दोर्भ्यां धृतो लीलया
तेन त्वं दिवि भूतले च सततं गोवर्धनोद्धारकः ।
त्वां त्रैलोक्यधरं वहामि कुचयोरग्रे न तद्गण्यते
किं वा केशव भाषणेन बहुना पुण्यैर्यशो लभ्यते ॥

This is what a gopi tells Krishna:
You are the one who lifted the Govardhan Mountain
The one in whose mouth Yashoda saw the universe.
But no one seems to count this
What is the use of mere talking; one earns fame and
becomes a celebrity only by merit

सन्ध्यावन्दन भद्रमस्तु भवते भोः स्नान तुभ्यं नमः
भो देवाः पितरश्च तर्पणविधौ नाहं क्षमः क्षम्यताम् ।

यत्र क्वापि निषिद्य यादवकुलोत्तंसस्य कंसद्विषः
स्मारं स्मारमघं हरामि तदलं मन्ये किमन्येन मे ॥

O sandhya vandana!
May all be well with you
O snana
I prostrate before you
O celestials and ancestors
Forgive me; I am incapable of performing tarpan for you
Sitting somewhere in a calm place and remembering the
stories and exploits of the jewel of the Yadu dynasty,
Krishna, I will dissolve all my sins
I think this is all I need to do, what else is
there for me to do?
The devotee who wants to remain forever consumed in
the remembrance of the leelas of the Lord.

Shabdavali
Meaning of Hindi and Sanskrit Words

A

Aarti sacred fire/worship

Abhisheka bathing

Agni fire

Aghori follower of black magic

Amrit nectar

Amavasya eclipse, dark moon lunar phase

Ashram abode

Ashtadhalam eight-pedalled lotus

Ashvamedha Yagna horse sacrifice, one of the most important royal rituals of Vedic religion

Ashtamangal auspicious

Avatar incarnation

B

Bael/Bilvam/Vilvam medium sized slender aromatic armed tree

Baanhi flute

Kela/vazhai maram banana cultivated primarily for their fruit, and to a lesser extent for the production of fibre and as ornamental plants

Bansuri flute

Bhakti worship

Bhaktamala Vaishnavite chanting beads

Bhasma ash

Bhoomi vandan salutation to Mother Earth

Bodhi wisdom

Brahmana the Brahmanas are part of the Hindu *śruti* literature. They are commentaries on the four Vedas, detailing the proper performance of rituals

Buddhi that faculty of the mind that is discriminative in nature which is able to discern truth from falsehood and which makes wisdom possible

C

Chakras "force centres" or whorls of energy permeating, from a point on the physical body, the layers of the subtle bodies in an ever-increasing fan-shaped formation

Charak Samhita the oldest ancient Sanskrit Ayurvedic text written perhaps in 600 BC

Charanamrit holy water served at temples and during puja mixed with Tulsi plant

Chaturmasya period of four months beginning on Shayani Ekadashi - the 11th day of the first bright half of Ashadh, the fourth month of the Hindu lunar calendar, until Prabodhini Ekadashi, the 11th day of the first bright half of the Kartik or the eighth month of the Hindu lunar calendar. It is believed that Hindu gods and goddesses are at rest. Chaturmas literally means four months.

Chunri fabric worn over head like a sari

D

Danava demon
Devi goddess
Devta god
Dharma justice

G

Gada mace
Garuda Lord Vishnu's eagle carrier
Gau mata mother cow
Gaushala cow home
Ghee ingredient of butter
Godaan the gift of a cow to a brahmana
Gopala cowherd
Gopi Lord Krishna's female friend
Gurukul School

J

Japa mala prayer beads
Jatismara one who remembers previous birth's
Jiva Agni life fire
Jivanmukta liberated while still in the physical body

K

Kanchan kaya youthfulness
Kalash pot

Kalpas an aeon or a long period of time in Hindu and Buddhist cosmology

Kapha Ayurveda

Karma "action" or "deed" or the cycle of cause and effect

Kartika eighth month of the Hindu lunar calendar

Kichad muddy water

Kumkum red powder

L

Lalla child

Linga penis of Lord Shiva

M

Mahavana forest in which Lord Krishna's birthplace, Gokula, is located

Muhurat auspicious time

Mangalsutra the necklace symbolising a married woman

Mantra chanting

Moksh salvation

Mudra hand movement

Murli flute

N

Naag serpent

Nakshatra the term for lunar mansion in Hindu astrology

Neem/Vepa Maram medical plant

Niyati destiny

O

Onam harvest festival

P

Padma lotus flower

Panchang a Hindu astrological almanac which follows traditional Indian cosmology

Panch Maha Yagna Five Great Yagnas or rituals (1. DevaYagna - Offerings to Lord 2. PitrYagna - Offering libations to ancestors' 3. BhutaYagna - Offering food to all departed souls 4. ManushyaYagna - Offerings to guests 5. BrahmaYagna - Reciting of the Vedas, namely Rigveda, Yajurveda, Samaveda and Atharvaveda)

Panch five

Pandit priest

Parmatma Almighty

Parampara ritual

Pativrata chastity

Prithvi earth

Purohit priest

Purshotam God

Pavan wind

Peepal/Arasu the tree below which Lord Krishna breathed his last

Prabhodani Ekadasi waking eleventh

Prana vital life

Prasad food blessed by the Gods

Prithvi earth

Puranas scriptures

R

Raaga note of meolody

Raashis house of planets

Rasayana prevention diseases and improving immunity and rejuvenation

Rishi hermit

Rudra anger

S

Sadh/Sayani Ekadasi "sleeping eleventh" when Lord Vishnu retires to sleep in a vast ocean on the back of his serpent Ananta

Sadhu seer

Sakha male friend

Sakhi female friend

Samadhi it is a meditative absorption or trance

Samudramanthana churning of the Ocean

Sandhya Vandan worship of Gods three times a day at the junctures of Night-Morning-afternoon-evening

Shabdam classical dance form

Sattva the energy of purity

Satvik ascetic

Sepoy soldier

Shaligrama name of a stone

Shankha conch

Sila stone

Siddhas offerings to a Brahmana

Sindoor vermillion

Sraddha funeral ceremonies

Surya Namaskar sun worship

Suvar pig

T

Tantrik one who practices black magic

Tapasya meditation

Teevramagan note in melody

Tirthas holy Rivers or pilgrimage

Tulabharam an incident in the life of Rukmini, which reveals the extent to which humble devotion, is worth more than material wealth.

Tulsi mritika earth beneath the Tulsi plant

Tulsi-mata mother plant

Tulsithara/Vrindavan seven circumambulations of the eight pedalled Tulsi plant

V

Vaikuntha heaven

Vardaan boon

Vata atmosphere

Vedic religious rituals

Vishnupriya beloved of Lord Vishnu

Vishwaas faith

Vivaah marriage

Y

Yajna fire God

Yama Lord of death

Names for Lord Krishna
with meanings

A

Achala – Still Lord

Adbhutah – Wonderful God

Aditya – The Son of Aditi

Ajava – The Conqueror of life and death

Amrut – Heavenly nectar ((no) = Mrut (Death))

Ananta – The Endless Lord

Aparajeet – The Lord Who Cannot Be Defeated

Achyuta – Infallible Lord

Adidev – The Original Lord

Ajanma – The Unborn

Akshara – Indestructible Lord

Anandsagar – Ocean of Transcendental Bliss

Anantajit – Ever Victorious Lord

Aniruddha – One Who Cannot be obstructed

Avyukta – One Who Is As Clear as Crystal

B

Bihari – The Travelling Lord

Balakrishna – The Child Krishna

Balagopala – The Child Krishna, the All Attractive

C

Chaturbhuja – Four – Armed Lord

D

Danavendra – Granter of Boons

Dayanidhi – The Compassionate Lord

Devakinandana – The Lord of Dharma

Dvarkapati – Protector of Dwarka

Dayalu – Repository of Compassion

Devadideva – The God of the Gods

Devesha – Lord of the Demigods

Dravin – The one who has no Enemies

G

Gopala – One Who Plays with the Cowherds

Govinda – One who pleases the Cows, Lands and Nature

Gopalpriya – Lover of Cowherds

Gyaneshwara – The Lord of Knowledge

H

Hiranyagarbha – Golden Womb (creator)

Hari – The Lord of Nature

Hrushikesha – The Lord of all Senses

J

Jagdisha – Lord of the Universe

Janardana – One who Bestows Boons on one and all

Jyotiraaditya – The resplendence of the Sun

K

Kamalanatha – The Lord of Goddess Lakshmi

Kamsantaka – Slayer of Kamsa

Keshava – One Who Has Long, Black Matted Locks

Kamalanayana – The Lord with Lotus Shaped Eyes

Kanjalochana – The lotus–eyed God

Krishna – All Attractive

L

Lakshmikaanta – The Lord of Goddess Lakshmi

Lokadhyaksha – Lord of all the three Worlds

M

Madhusudan – Slayer of Demon Madhu

Manmohna – Bewildering the Mind

Mayura – The Lord who has a Peacock Feathered-Crest

Murali – The Flute Playing Lord

Muralimanohara – The Lord who enchants with Flute play

Madana – The Lord of Love

Madhava – Husband to Goddess of Fortune

Mahendra – Lord of Indra

Manohara – Beautiful Lord

Mohnish – Attractive God

Muralidhar – One who holds the flute

N

Nandakumara – Son of Nanda

Nandagopala – The loved cowherd

Navanitachora – Thief of Butter

Nirguna – Without any Material Properties

Narayana – The Refuge of Everyone

Niranjana – The Unblemished Lord

P

Padmahasta – One who has hands like lotus

Parampurusha – Supreme Enjoyer

Parabrahmana – The Supreme Absolute Truth

Prajapati – Lord of all creatures

Padmanabha – The Lord who has a lotus in the navel

Paramatma – Charioteer of Partha (Arjun)

Punyah – Achieved by penance

Purshottama – The Supreme Soul

R

Ravilochana – One Whose Eye is the Sun

S

Sahasraaksah – Thousand – Eyed Lord

Sakshi – All witnessing Lord

Sarvajana – Omniscient Lord

Sarveshwara – Master of All

Sarvapalaka – Protector of all

Satyavachana – One who speaks only the Truth

Shantah – Peaceful Lord

Shrikanta, Srikanta – Beautiful Lord

Shyamasundara – Lord of the Beautiful Evenings

Sumedha – Intelligent Lord

Svargapati – Lord of Heavens

Satyavrata – The Truthful Vow

Shreshhtha – The Most Glorious Lord

Shyam – Dark Complexioned Lord

Sudarshana – Handsome Lord

Suresham – Lord of all Demi-Gods

T

Trivikrama – Conqueror of all the three Worlds

U

Upendra – Brothers of Indra

V

Vaikunthanatha – Lord of Vaikuntha, the Heavenly Abode

Vasudevaputra – Son of King Vasudeva

Vishwadakshinah – Skilful and Efficient Lord

Vishwamurti – Of the form of the Entire Universe

Vishwatma – Soul of the Universe

Vardhamaanah – The Formless Lord

Vishnu – All Prevailing Lord, Lord of the Universe, as Vishwa means Universe

Vishwakarma – Creator of the Universe

Lists & References

Vedas & Scriptures
Soundarya Lahari
Bhagavad Gita
Bhaja Govindam
Sri Harivamsa Purana
Vishnu Purana
Samkshipt Padma Purana
Varaha Purana
Bhagavata Purana
Brahma Purana
Skanda Purana
Lalitha Sahasranamam
Sri Krishna Karnamrutham
Sri Krishna Ashtakam
Hari Bhakti Vilasa
Vishnu Sahasranamam
Narayaneeyam
Tulasi Stotram
Sri Bhaktamala
Sri Suktam

Weapons cannot pierce

through this soul and fire

cannot burn it. Water cannot

drench it and the wind cannot

dry it. The soul is eternal

and therefore cannot be

damaged, burnt, drowned.

It is ageless, timeless

and therefore eternal.

—Lord Krishna

BHAWANA SOMAAYA has been a journalist for almost 40 years. She is a film critic, columnist, and author of 14 books and they are a point of reference for students studying cinema at Whistling Woods, Manipal University, and now JNU, Delhi.

She has served on Advisory Panel of Film Certificate in India and is currently the Entertainment Editor at 92.7 Big FM Radio channel.

Somaaya's Krishna: The God who lived as Man released in 2008. Keshava: A Magnificent Obsession is her second offering to the deity.

Somaaya was conferred with the Padma Shri in 2017.